THE BAD MISS BENNET ABROAD

After George Wickham's untimely demise on the battlefield at Waterloo, merry widow Lydia Wickham, née Bennet, is in want of a rich husband. Failing to find one in Europe, she embarks on a voyage to Brazil accompanied by her trusty maid, Adelaide, to join the exiled Portuguese Court in Rio de Janeiro. She soon catches the eye of the heir, Dom Pedro. Staying out of trouble doesn't come naturally to Lydia, as she is captured by pirates, then makes a second disastrous marriage, and even finds ways to ruin the Darcys' tranquil existence all over again. Will she ever succeed in her quest for "an agreeable husband with an estate and two matching footmen", or will her taste for adventure lead her astray once more?

SPECIAL MESSAGE TO READERS

THE ULVERSCROFT FOUNDATION
(registered UK charity number 264873)
was established in 1972 to provide funds for
research, diagnosis and treatment of eye diseases.
Examples of major projects funded by
the Ulverscroft Foundation are:-

- The Children's Eye Unit at Moorfields Eye Hospital, London
- The Ulverscroft Children's Eye Unit at Great Ormond Street Hospital for Sick Children
- Funding research into eye diseases and treatment at the Department of Ophthalmology, University of Leicester
- The Ulverscroft Vision Research Group, Institute of Child Health
- Twin operating theatres at the Western Ophthalmic Hospital, London
- The Chair of Ophthalmology at the Royal Australian College of Ophthalmologists

You can help further the work of the Foundation
by making a donation or leaving a legacy.
Every contribution is gratefully received. If you
would like to help support the Foundation or
require further information, please contact:

THE ULVERSCROFT FOUNDATION
**The Green, Bradgate Road, Anstey
Leicester LE7 7FU, England
Tel: (0116) 236 4325**

website: www.foundation.ulverscroft.com

THE BAD MISS BENNET ABROAD

JEAN BURNETT

LARGE
PRINT

First published in Great Britain 2016
by
Canelo Digital Publishing Limited

First Isis Edition
published 2017

A catalogue record for this book is available
from the British Library.

ISBN 978–1–78541–405–3 (hb)
ISBN 978–1–78541–411–4 (pb)

Published by
F. A. Thorpe (Publishing)
Anstey, Leicestershire

Set by Words & Graphics Ltd.
Anstey, Leicestershire
Printed and bound in Great Britain by
T. J. International Ltd., Padstow, Cornwall

This book is printed on acid-free paper

Part One

Prologue

I have never had much luck with lovers or husbands. Most of my difficulties since the age of sixteen have been due to an unerring talent for choosing the wrong man, coupled with a lack of money. The two things are, of course, closely connected in a woman's life. Ladies, beware of the allure of a uniform — especially if a comely man is inside.

After the less than heroic death of Wickham at Waterloo I returned to England and made my way to Pemberley, where I hoped for comfort and support from my sister Lizzie and her husband. Instead, I found Mr Darcy intent on marrying me off to the nearest curate — a fate not to be borne. After some unpleasantness I escaped to London to join my friends.

What a trio we were — Selena and Miles Caruthers and Lydia Bennet Wickham. Our escapades were the greatest fun and garnered us a satisfactory amount of money, although it lasted an immoderately short time. I did not lack for admirers in London but, as always, they were either unsuccessful, disreputable or downright criminal (a highwayman), and sometimes all three at the same time.

My involvement with one of these gentlemen led me to Brighton and the Prince Regent's bedroom while at the same time embroiling me in affairs of state — for which I have no inclination or talent. Fortunately, a friend obtained an invitation to Almack's ballroom for me. At the time I regarded this as the greatest good fortune I had enjoyed in my entire life. It would, I was sure, compensate for my unfortunate marriage to Mr Wickham — although I was only sixteen at the time, dear reader, and with little knowledge of men and their wicked ways.

Miles told me, "We expect you to catch a duke at the very least." Indeed, if one could not do so at Almack's, where else could it be done? This place was where the *ton* met and found suitable partners — and occasionally unsuitable ones. I hoped to meet a man who would provide me with marriage, respectability, a small but comfortable estate (not entailed), a matching footman or two and a diamond or three. In short, I had the legitimate aspirations of any refined young woman. Surely I deserved such a fate? Not quite twenty years old I was already a widow — a penniless widow, as Mr Darcy often reminded me.

The Austrian Count who beguiled me at the ballroom might have been the answer to my prayers. He invited me to accompany him to Paris (Paris!), another ambition realised — but sadly it transpired that he already had a wife. My dreams were shattered but, as my maid Adelaide reminded me, women have few choices and must take the rough with the smooth.

Realising the truth of this I agreed to the arrangement, taking care not to give the details to my family when I returned for a stay at Pemberley. I made the mistake of confiding all in a letter to my silly sister Kitty, who betrayed me by sending the letter to Mr Darcy. The repercussions from this were most painful and, in short, I was dispatched by my brother-in-law to be a companion to an old lady in Bath.

How quickly one can descend from the heights to the depths! It seemed but a wink of an eye from dancing in my finery at Almack's to dragging an obnoxious pug called Wellington across the Bath downland at the behest of Mrs Makepeace, my employer.

However, the gods of fortune had not turned away from me entirely. Mrs Makepeace proved to be a most amiable lady who often recounted to me her adventures in pre-revolutionary Paris before Napoleon ruined everything. An idea germinated in my mind. I would persuade my employer somehow to end her reclusive existence and venture to the continent again — and I succeeded. We embarked for France in due course.

When we reached Paris my life was further complicated by a certain Captain Marshfield, an aide to the Duke of Wellington. He knew about my adventures in Brighton where I had helped (accidentally) to recover the Prince Regent's jewels known as the Cambridge emeralds. In short, I was enlisted in the service of His Majesty's Government as an occasional spy, aided by my maid, Adelaide, who has far more ability in this area than I. The captain's presence slightly overshadowed my enjoyment of the Palais Royal and such delicacies as grilled pigs' trotters *a la Francais*, but life is never perfect.

Eventually, Mrs Makepeace wished to move on to Venice and we set off on our travels once more. I was not greatly taken with the Water City which was somewhat down at heel and green and mouldy around the edges at that time. Captain Marshfield once again dogged our footsteps but I took solace in the knowledge that my hero, Lord Byron, was living in a palace on the Grand Canal. I planned to meet him if I could distract the captain and my employer for a few hours.

I donned a cape and a mask, Venetian style, and wandered around the alleyways and squares and along the banks of the canals. My maid, Adelaide, had become involved with a baker called Vittorio. She dallied with him on occasions and brought back delicious pastries and breads. The baker's wife, La Fornarina, was very beautiful and was, I discovered, the mistress of Lord Byron. When his lordship tired of her she returned home and became insanely jealous of Adelaide. She was a tempestuous woman.

"The women of Brighton are pussy cats compared with her," Adelaide announced gloomily and took to creeping about, glancing over her shoulder constantly.

Our time in Venice came to an abrupt and melancholy conclusion. Lord Byron and I were destined to meet, but in unfortunate circumstances. One morning Mrs Makepeace, Adelaide, Wellington and I were rowed out into the lagoon in the gondola by Tito, our hired gondolier. As we returned to the Grand Canal we spied a swimmer.

6

"Yes, it is the English milord," Tito confirmed. Byron's swimming was legendary. Overcome with excitement I leaned too far over the side of the vessel and tumbled into the water. When I surfaced, freezing and terrified, I hoped that Lord Byron would be on hand to rescue me, but Tito hauled me aboard with the pole while my hero showed little interest.

Once on board I found that Wellington had mysteriously disappeared — thrown overboard? Both Adelaide and Tito disliked the dog. Meanwhile, Mrs Makepeace lay very still on her cushions having expired from shock! Once again, dear reader, the fates had conspired against me. I was not greatly diverted.

When I returned once more to England I was delighted to be re-united with dear Selena and Miles, and even more delighted to discover that my former employer had left me a sizeable amount of money as well as her pearls. At last I was of independent means and could make my own way as I pleased. I had great pleasure in relaying news of my good fortune before I travelled to Pemberley.

"You are remarkably accident prone, madam," remarked my brother-in-law when we met again. Lizzie reproached him for his heartless remark — a most satisfactory state of affairs. I should have guessed that Mr Darcy would not desist from his attempts to marry me off. Once again a suitable curate was dangled before me, and this time I decided to have a little enjoyment at Mr Darcy's expense. I had already planned to re-join the count in Paris but I gave the impression that I would accept Mr Arbuthnot, the curate. Guests arrived at Pemberley ... and, in short, there were many misunderstandings and plots gone awry which I thoroughly enjoyed before Adelaide and I made our escape.

Once again installed in Paris I enjoyed a touching reunion with the count, who informed me that we had been invited to stay with the exiled Caroline, Princess of Wales. Off we went to the Villa Caprile in Italy with Captain Marshfield's orders ringing in my ears. I was to report back on the princess' activities as well as the count's.

My sojourn at the villa would have been charming in many ways had I not been obliged to spy on everyone. The princess was most gracious to me and we enjoyed swimming and amateur dramatics in the warm sunshine. I reported back on the various schemes afoot in the villa, using the egg man as courier. The Prince Regent was anxious for a divorce and wanted to gather as much ammunition as possible against his estranged wife.

Count Esterhazy and I eventually tired of each other and he insisted on leaving for Vienna. We made our farewells to the princess and on the journey he became extremely evasive about our plans, saying only that he had a "grand future" planned for me. Adelaide warned me that this did not bode well. She has a nose for these things but my optimistic nature caused me to hope for good news.

And so it transpired, dear reader, that once more I should be deceived by a man in whom I had placed my trust and affection. The future planned for me was as an extra lady-in-waiting to the Hapsburg princess, the

Archduchess Leopoldina, who was betrothed to the heir to the Portuguese throne.

"It will be a grand adventure," I told Adelaide. "We will be in a royal household — what an advancement for me! Also, I have never visited Portugal. No doubt it is a charming place."

Adelaide looked doubtful, as well she might. I had forgotten that the entire Portuguese court had decamped to their vast colony on the other side of the world in order to escape the invasion of Portugal by Napoleon. They had stayed on there and appeared to have no plans to return to Europe. Leopoldina and I were destined for Brazil.

The shock and horror this news inspired in me cannot be adequately described. I was forced to have recourse to the laudanum bottle on several occasions and even the provision of a new wardrobe did little to pacify me or raise my spirits. The Archduchess was charming and gracious and assured me my duties would be light. Chiefly, I was to make conversation in English with her. The real ladies-in-waiting were all aristocrats and seldom deigned to talk to me.

The journey to Brazil would take almost six months — at sea! What a fearsome prospect. Would I ever see my native land again? I had been contracted for two years but that was meaningless. I might well fall prey to a ghastly tropical disease, or the ship would sink or as Adelaide said, "We will be captured by pirates and sold to the Sultan of Tartary or some such person. Where is Brazil?" she added. "Is it near Australia?" I nodded. We both collapsed on the sofa and sobbed. I was only slightly consoled to learn that large diamonds were easily found in Brazil. Adelaide asked whether they grew on trees.

Before we embarked on a huge ship heavily laden with people, animals, furniture and treasure (barely seaworthy), Captain Marshfield was again at my door urging me to send dispatches back from Rio de Janeiro. I turned a deaf ear, doubting that the need would ever arise.

Adelaide and I were obliged to make elaborate preparations for the journey. We assembled clothes suitable for the ferocious climate and as much medicine as possible. Mrs Makepeace's gold coins were placed in a stout trunk. As the heavily laden ship slowly made its way out to sea I stood on deck watching Europe recede into the mist. Adelaide had already turned green and had retired below with a supply of ginger.

A member of the crew tapped me on the shoulder and suggested I might like to retire below. I turned and beheld Jerry Sartain, one of the disreputable and criminal people who had crossed my path, as mentioned earlier. He was also the one who had truly captured my heart. I have always loved unwisely but too well, dear reader. In fact, Jerry had been a highwayman when we first met — on that occasion he was robbing my coach in Epping Forest. Despite this inauspicious introduction I would have done anything for him.

He had eventually boarded a ship to the New World in order to escape the gallows in England and now we were to be together all the way to Brazil. I was forced to grab the ship's handrail in order to control my emotions. Interesting times lay ahead.

CHAPTER
ONE

September 10th, 1817

We have been swaying around on this dreadful vessel, vomiting and bewailing our lot for twenty-one days since our departure in August, in this year of grace 1817. As I write this in my journal my maid is muttering in the background; "This is a coffin ship."

It is not quite that: Adelaide has a tendency to exaggerate. Our plight is best described as being imprisoned in a cell with its bare stone walls hidden with a velvet cover, but a cell, nevertheless, smelling badly and constantly moving. The captain of this prison keeps a brightly coloured parrot in similar circumstances.

Not that the cramped cabin I share with Adelaide boasts much in the way of velvet covers. My maid attempts to make it more comfortable with the linens and coverlets taken from our trunks, but after a few weeks at sea with little or no washing facilities the place has become somewhat foetid. During the frequent bouts of bad weather the entire ship leaks. It is scarcely to be borne.

I have become salt-encrusted in soul and body. The sanitary arrangements at sea are not to be thought of, as far as possible. I am not much troubled by sea sickness but the entire Portuguese contingent is prone to vomit with every roll of the waves — surprising behaviour from such a stout, seafaring people. My royal employer, Dona Leopoldina, is not affected. "We must maintain self-control at all times," she admonishes us.

Thank heavens for my duties with the princess, varied by the distractions provided by Jerry Sartain's presence on the ship. I often recall with mixed emotions our previous encounters in England. My plight, otherwise, would be unendurable.

At dinner last night the captain announced, "I expect this voyage to last for another seventy-five days at least, due to the constant bad weather." He waved a bottle of cognac at the parrot while cries of dismay rose from the ladies, accompanied by a severe lurching of the ship. Several wine decanters upended their contents in sympathy.

Our meals on board ship invariably end in this way; sometimes they even start in the same mode. People rushed to assist the princess before her gown became soaked in red wine. She gave a brave smile and the captain's parrot — always present — uttered several loud profanities in English which, fortunately, the Portuguese ladies did not understand. Jerry told me later that the parrot had done long service on a British man-of-war.

I am learning an entire new vocabulary from this bird. I release my pent-up feelings of rage and despair by repeating the words softly to myself when I am alone in my cabin. Adelaide told me that she does the same thing.

My highwayman, who must now be known as my sailor, or as Adelaide calls him, my jolly Jack Tar, meets me whenever he can. He pops out from behind a cable or a cannon, or emerges from a hatch below deck in an unnerving manner. I find his presence most discombobulating.

"You must not accost me in this way," I reproved him. "We may be seen by the chief lady-in-waiting and I shall be ruined. She hates me, you know." Jerry was as unsympathetic as ever.

"What can they do to you, my sweet? We are at sea. They can scarcely throw you overboard."

Another intolerable thought occurred to me. "If they are displeased with me, my contract might be terminated when we reach Brazil. I could be put on a ship back to England immediately." This prospect made me grow faint and did not prevent him from seizing me around the waist in a sticky, salty embrace.

"Be brave, *mon vieux!*" he whispered in execrable French, before disappearing behind a water tank. Weak at the knees, I made my way to Dona Leopoldina's apartment.

You will notice that I did not refer to her living area as a cabin. Sixty cannon have been removed from the ship's decks to make way for her splendid quarters. The lady was watching disconsolately as servants wedged packing cases around her grand piano to prevent it from rolling around due to the worsening weather. She gave me a listless smile.

"Even the consolations of Bach and Mozart are denied me in this situation," she sighed. "A piano is of little use at present." Indeed, I would willingly have exchanged the piano for more salubrious sanitary arrangements, but I did not voice my opinion. "Shall we study my botanical drawings?" the princess invited, opening a gilt-embossed leather volume before frowning again. "Later we will have to visit the heads." I repressed a groan. The "heads" consist of a platform fastened to the bow and suspended over the ship's wake. This is where all the passengers queue to relieve themselves into the ocean. It is a frightful experience, although the area is cleared when the princess appears.

I stared at a sketch of the Great Bustard. "It is extinct," the princess remarked. I was not greatly diverted.

"Shall I call some of the musicians, Your Highness?" I asked in an attempt to lighten the mood. The lady's eyes brightened and two fiddlers were soon summoned to play some lively airs during a blissful hour of calm weather. As rays of sunshine penetrated the roof window of the salon our spirits rose a little. Through a half opened door I caught a glimpse of the royal bedchamber, full of gold plated pitchers and bowls and red and white silk decorations.

Despite this grandeur, life at sea was taking as great a toll on the princess' appearance as it was on her attendants. She is not as soignée as of late. Real finesse is impossible in a constantly swaying environment. Similarly she could not avoid the occasional wafts of stinking air that emerged from the hold where dozens of animals are kept — enough to fill a zoo. At times we heard other noises as the poor creatures were executed to provide our dinner.

After the musicians left, we turned our attention to our Portuguese grammar books. Dona Leopoldina caught sight of one of the few novels I have been able to bring on board, *Glenarvon* by Lady Caroline Lamb. It is a thinly disguised account of dear Lord Byron and a great favourite of mine.

The princess frowned at the title and told me that I "should not read any literature that excited passion and sensuality." When I glanced at her coiffure she pulled at the stray tendrils and added that, "we should also avoid long and scandalous toilettes." It saddened me to see this young woman, so privileged yet so weighed down by expectations and duties, mouthing sentiments I would have expected to hear from my self-righteous brother-in-law, Mr Darcy, or my sister Mary.

Scandalous books and toilettes are among the greatest pleasures life has to offer and both are in short supply on this ship. I murmured an agreement as the vessel started to roll again. It was time for our visit to the heads followed by a break for refreshments. The ship has an evil mind of its own, always reserving its worst behaviour for these two events — or was it the elements at fault? My brain is becoming addled, probably by salt.

"At least you are not surviving on hard tack and rum," Jerry grumbled when we met later that day. "You cannot imagine the conditions below deck while you are swanning around in the royal salon." Speechless, I pointed to my salt-dried hair and limp muslins which Adelaide had unsuccessfully attempted to revive with a little lavender water.

"As you can see, conditions for ladies at sea are especially difficult," I protested. "You men do not object to a lack of soap and water, for the most part. I agree that your rations must be poor but you have rum to blot out everything when necessary." This argument did not prevail with him and ended with a promise from me to smuggle out a chicken leg or two.

"It's nothing but rum, sodomy and the lash for the crew," he muttered, as he disappeared below deck.

Why do our encounters always end in capitulation on my part? Our relationship is so problematic. How far am I from my dearest ambition — marriage to an amiable gentleman of means with a country estate and two matching footmen? I am unlikely to meet such a person in darkest Brazil. As for the Austrian noblemen on board, they are as stiff as boards and I have had enough of their ways.

Back in my cabin I started to write a letter to my dear friend, Selena. My news will be stale indeed after it travels for six months across the Atlantic. I dared not mention Jerry's presence on board. All I could say was that Dona Leopoldina dreaded meeting her mother-in-law.

"Who doesn't?" Adelaide remarked when I read this aloud.

Dinner that evening ended in chaos once more. At one point the ship keeled over completely onto one side. Chairs were upended, wine spilled and plates and glasses shattered. The Portuguese ladies descended into hysterics, the men shouted, the parrot cursed, and even the princess shed a tear. At least I would have something exciting to tell Selena. When the ship righted itself members of the crew arrived to carry us to our quarters. Jerry was not among them, I noted.

CHAPTER
TWO

October 23rd

Will we arrive in Brazil in this decade or the next? The never-ending voyage continues. Perhaps we are heading for Australia, the far side of the world. Certainly I am beginning to feel like a convict bound for a penal colony, but I must not fall into melancholy and exaggeration. If I am a convict then I am a privileged one. The ship is so overcrowded that many people are forced to sleep on deck. There is a system of rotation, I understand, where Austrian noblemen share the cabin accommodation.

"One of the ladies-in-waiting has suffered an infestation of lice," I told Adelaide. "Her head has been shaved and powdered and she now wears a strange-looking turban to cover her baldness." We sniggered a good deal over this but our merriment soon ceased when we realised that this plague could spread to others. My hair is my best feature and the thought of losing it fills me with dread.

"You should avoid too much contact with sailor Jerry, madam," Adelaide advised. "All them sailors are rancid at best due to their conditions below decks. You might catch all manner of nasties." She is right of course. I shall use this as an excuse to avoid becoming intimately involved with him. I must avoid scandal at all costs.

The Countess of K, chief lady-in-waiting, persecutes me whenever she can. I am subjected to long, boring lectures on Viennese court etiquette, which seem pointless as we are no longer in Vienna. The countess already looks back with nostalgia to a golden age compared to the tropical nightmare awaiting us in Brazil.

"The Portuguese are a backward people compared to the scientifically advanced Austrians," she announced. I reminded her that the English were the most advanced in that sphere but she waved away the notion.

"Napoleon was right about one thing. The English are a nation of shopkeepers." She is careful not to express any of these views in Dona Leopoldina's hearing. As for my poor self, I know nothing of correct behaviour due to my lowly origins. The countess gives me a sly pinch whenever she passes, just to confirm my status.

Our only amusement is in listening to the gossip about the court in Rio, filtered through several languages from the Portuguese who have visited already.

It is eccentric in the extreme: in the ten years since the court removed from Lisbon it has embraced an almost oriental decadence, crossed with medieval European practices long abandoned, even by our own peculiar House of Hanover. The king's mother, Queen

Maria, recently died totally insane, but our poor King George is also mad. It must be a royal affliction.

Dona Carlota, the dreaded mother-in-law of Dona Leopoldina, is Spanish and loathed by everyone. She is known as the "Witch of Cordoba." She is very small, very ugly, unruly and contentious and interested only in Andalusian dancing and horses. It is rumoured that her second son, Don Miguel, is not her husband's offspring. The royal couple separated and they now maintain their own households.

All this reaches the ears of poor Dona Leopoldina who is very Germanic, placid and serious in her disposition. I dread to think how she will fare in that tropical broth. At least I have only two years to serve, and several long months have passed already. If the return voyage lasts as long I may be grey-haired by the time I see England again.

"Never mind, madam," Adelaide remarked. "At least you will be a diamond-covered spinster." She is very little comfort sometimes. As for the diamonds — how many will come my way? The prospect of being alone as I grow older is beginning to oppress me. I am only two and twenty but many would consider me past my prime, especially as I am a widow.

I was taking a little exercise on deck when Jerry appeared. He leaped nimbly out of the way as the five children of the King's Commissioner scampered by, pursued by nursemaids and tutors. They were followed by more servants bearing pots of waving greenery and cages full of European and tropical birds, all needing their daily airing.

"This place is like Vauxhall Gardens!" he muttered, as we were both pressed against a stanchion. I am immoderately sick of this ship.

November 1st

Good fortune at last! The ship is now bearing down towards Salvador de Bahia in northern Brazil. Our destination is in sight. We have been beguiled with promises of fresh water and tropical fruits and fine new gowns kept especially for this event. Very grand preparations have been made to welcome the princess, and her ladies must look their best. We will be able to remove the salt from our persons and even Dona Leopoldina will not object to a few scandalous toilettes.

"I shall be taking my leave of the ship as soon as we arrive in Rio," Jerry told me. "The sea-going life is not for me. I had no choice in the matter, being a wanted man. There are riches to be grasped from the fertile lands in Brazil's interior and I intend to get my share." His vision includes becoming a sugar grower with many slaves, enlisting as a soldier of fortune, or stumbling upon a diamond mine. I pointed out that he did not speak the language but he laughed at this. "I still have my sword and pistol stowed away. They speak louder than any language."

I heaved a sigh.

We both know that our future paths must diverge, but part of me wanted desperately to cry out, "Take me with you!" I would have given every Portuguese gold coin promised to me in exchange for a life with my bold highwayman, although I know that it could not possibly happen. Lydia Bennet Wickham could not survive in a pitiless tropical jungle without the amenities of civilised society and I fear that Jerry might consider me a burden. I heaved another sigh as he wandered off to the far reaches of the ship.

How did I become involved with a highwayman? I often ask this question of myself. Jerry and his accomplice robbed me of my jewellery on the coach journey to London after I had left Pemberley. When I spied him at the theatre with his doxy wearing my jewels, I gave chase and circumstances ended with the two of us becoming very intimately acquainted.

I must cease these reminiscences. I am not lucky with gentlemen, as Adelaide often reminds me. Jerry, however, is no gentleman.

CHAPTER
THREE

November 20th

Today I am writing in my new journal again, for you cannot imagine, dear reader, the excitement I felt as the ship slowly entered the enormous and magnificent Bay of Guanabara, with its strangely shaped mountain known as the Sugar Loaf. It was November 5th or 6th — dates have become difficult to remember, but the fireworks and cannon shots exploding above us seemed appropriate for the date, an exotic version of a Guy Fawkes celebration on a very large scale. Flags were waving and hundreds of small boats rowed by handsome dark youths, almost naked, came out to greet us. The ladies were agog as these young gods handed up unfamiliar fruit, *pitangas*, Jack fruit and *pupunhas*, which are like peaches.

Noise and colour and heat — thus began my time in Brazil. The delight and the horror, the beauty and the misery could not be a greater contrast from my well-ordered little homeland. I know that my stay here will be a great adventure. Longbourn is a distant memory. I have travelled across the world — and what will become of me?

Only two ladies-in-waiting were allowed to accompany Dona Leopoldina onto the golden barge which carried the royal family. The rest of us watched from the deck as the newlywed couple eyed each other furtively under lowered eyelids. The dark looks of the heir to the throne, Dom Pedro, contrasted sharply with her blonde, blue-eyed appearance. The marriage had been celebrated by proxy in Vienna.

I thought I would die of pleasure when I felt *terra firma* beneath my feet again. We disembarked on the following day when we joined a procession of ninety carriages through the streets of Rio, which were decorated as if for a Roman carnival. My senses were overwhelmed by the shouting, screaming, cannon fire and fireworks combined with military bands and oven heat. The vastness of my surroundings and the huge crowds disoriented my senses and I became faint, grabbing the carriage window for support.

"This place is smelly," pronounced Adelaide when we surveyed our rooms in the São Cristovão palace. "That dung heap should go." She pointed to the pile of manure just observable from the window over which thousands of insects hovered. "Just our luck to be quartered so close to the thing . . . and the floors are dirty, *and* the tapestries are filthy . . ."

"I know, I know," I agreed, "but there is little we can do." Standards of cleanliness are not high at court. Indeed, after the pomp and ceremony of our arrival the palace is a disappointment, an undistinguished building lacking in style or order. Pemberley is far more impressive. Adelaide is fully occupied in trying to get fresh water for bathing and washing my clothes. Her requests are met by a languid wave of the hand and instruction to "tell the slaves to fetch it."

In contrast to the almost dingy palace, there is a staff of thousands — mostly black slaves who vastly outnumber the Portuguese. They are treated very badly and are constantly whipped. I know that some people in England keep black servants but the British government is now trying to abolish slavery everywhere.

The court officials have assigned a slave to me. I insisted that I did not need one as I had my own servant but they did not appear to understand. The girl's name is Eufrasia; her skin is as black as coal and as smooth as marble. She stares at me with veiled, impenetrable eyes and she speaks no English. Adelaide is up in arms thinking that I would have no further use for her but I reassured her on that score.

"You know I could not manage without your help," I told her. "Let Eufrasia do the heavier work as she is accustomed to the heat." I was also given a whip which I threw out in disgust. The girl watched me do this, her face impassive. We will manage by sign language and some basic Portuguese words.

Eufrasia brings me my daily breakfast of manioc meal in coconut milk with fried bananas or guavas, or other tropical fruits. The manioc meal is not vastly different from porridge and I have become accustomed to it. The tropical fruits are delicious and a blessing after the long months without such things. Often we drink a strange tasting beverage called *guaraná*.

When I was presented to the king, Dom João VI, he appeared to be a kindly, gracious man but I noticed immediately that he seldom washed. This was apparent from his bodily odour, heavily overlaid with strong perfumes. When I was required to kiss his hand I noticed another unpleasant aroma in the room. Could it be ... surely not? A scandalised Austrian lady confirmed it — the king kept overflowing chamber pots in the corners of his receiving room.

The Portuguese logic is that as the upper classes never touch anything dirty, they do not need to wash. The Cariocas, the natives of Rio, on the other hand, are very clean people who wash and bathe daily.

"They've gone native, you know, except for the cleanliness aspect." My fellow countryman was referring to the court and the royal family. We were standing on a veranda watching a tropical twilight glinting gold and copper on the horizon. Within minutes it faded into grey and then black as an all-enveloping velvet cloak. "The bat's wing of night," said my companion quite poetically.

I had found a large contingent of British people established in Rio to secure our interests in trade and foreign affairs. When I was allowed to leave the palace I was often invited into their homes.

Mr Luccombe is a textile merchant from London, who has made a fortune during his ten years in the country. The British have a monopoly on trade to Brazil and our goods pour into Rio daily. He keeps several slaves in his household but has not completely abandoned European ways. He assured me that anything I wanted from home could be brought in on the packet ship that sails from Falmouth every month.

"How do you find them at court, my dear?" he asked. "The king lives more like an oriental pasha than a Christian monarch, does he not, except for his aversion to washing?" The expatriates were all agog when they discovered that an Englishwoman had been appointed to a court position. I did not feel I could give them the real reason for my role.

"I confess I am wearied by the feudal customs and the long church services that I am required to attend, even though I am an Anglican," I replied. Mr Luccombe went on eagerly: "What do you think of the virago Carlota and Dom Pedro — a real Jack-the-Lad that one? There is always scandal about his mistresses. There was the French ballerina who had his child and . . ."

"Hush, John!" Mrs Luccombe interrupted her husband's unruly revelations with some embarrassment. Not in the least subdued, he assured us all that "a well-ordered, democratic society needs a temperate climate if it is to function well. I have tried to introduce the game of cricket in an attempt to civilise the locals." I gathered that this project had met with only moderate success.

Mrs Luccombe asked me if I cared for *guaraná*. "The locals regard it as almost the elixir of life and I confess I have become quite addicted to it," she told me.

"It bucks her up," her husband added with a broad smile. "The ladies find the climate very wearing."

We retreated into the house in an attempt to avoid the torment of the mosquitoes. I could not tell them that Dom Pedro had already shown some interest in me, giving hot, speaking glances in my direction whenever we were in the same room. When I told Adelaide about this, her reply was typically sharp.

"He does that to anything in skirts, it's well-known." She seldom offers me any sympathy, but I have no other confidante in the palace who can speak English. She always has an ear for the latest gossip, even in foreign languages. "There was the French ballerina . . ."

"Yes, I know about her."

"Then there was the wife of the captain of the royal guard."

"I do not want to have this conversation, Adelaide. We must not lose all sense of the niceties of civilised living." I knew how hypocritical I sounded, as I recalled the incident with the Prince Regent. From the expression on her face I could tell that my maid was remembering the same thing. However, once started on this theme I could not stop.

"We must remember that we are British," I added. "We come from a reassuring, well-ordered country, and we know the importance of linings." Adelaide looked puzzled.

"I am referring to the Brazilian habit of wearing almost transparent clothing which must add to the general decadence."

My maid gave me a shrewd look. "The French do that too, and so will you in this heat." She flounced off with the laundry basket and I wondered why I had bothered with that little speech. Obviously I was trying to put temptation behind me. I could not afford another scandal. As for my maid, Mama always said that we should set an example to the lower orders, but I fear I have not succeeded with Adelaide.

January 2nd, 1818

I am finding the adjustment to life in Rio a difficult one. The heat and the mosquitoes are insufferable. When we attended a ball given by an Austrian official, the ladies in their low-cut muslin gowns were so badly bitten that our shoulders were red raw, as if we had been whipped.

When the royal party entered the ballroom I was in attendance on Dona Leopoldina, although very much in the rear of the party due to my lowly status. Nevertheless, Dom Pedro singled me out, much to my discomfiture. His excuse was that he "wished to meet the only English lady at court." Dona Leopoldina presented me and I made my curtsey. Her husband puffed out his chest and licked his full lips before kissing my hand. His heavy lidded eyes spoke of sensuality and not a great deal of wit or intelligence.

"I speak little English", he apologised, "and my wife says that my French is even worse." He glanced roguishly at her and she responded with a strained smile.

"You must learn to speak Portuguese well, my dear, and then we can converse. You may tell me all about

England." I curtsied again and he moved on. I had been put totally out of countenance by being favoured so openly. The other ladies-in-waiting were giving me barbed looks. The Countess of K prodded me sharply in the ribs as the procession rounded a corner of the room. Later, Dom Pedro contrived to pinch my rear, while pretending to deal with a mosquito bite.

Many of the men were hopping up and down scratching at their silk stockings. It was oven hot indoors and scarcely better outside. Unlike on the European continent, the heat did not lessen at night. Oh, for those Italian nights I spent at the Princess of Wales' villa! Was it only a year ago? I wrenched my mind away from my time with the Austrian Count and its subsequent disasters. When I returned to my rooms, I tore off my underskirts and had recourse to Gowland's lotion.

I visit the homes of the British residents whenever possible as an antidote to the stiff ways of the court, but occasionally I am invited into a Portuguese dwelling. I visited the home of a certain Dona Gabriela de Castro, who wished to show off her command of English. Her house was furnished in an elegant style with many English objects, china and glassware and linens, together with French furniture. The ladies of the household busied themselves with embroidery and much nibbling of Portuguese pastries.

"How are you finding life in Rio, Senhora Wickham?" asked Dona Gabriela, as she casually threw pieces of cake onto the floor. I was too astonished to answer as I watched several black infants scrabbling around for the morsels. They were the children of the slave women of the household, who stood silently ranged around the walls. We discussed the domestic life of the city while I endeavoured to hide my surprise. When I noticed a long whip, standing ready in one corner of the room, I could scarcely contain my horror.

Summoning up my courage, I asked Senhora Gabriela if she had recourse to the whip often. She frowned, saying, "My slaves are docile for the most part but occasionally I whip one as an example to the others." She laughed at the shocked look I could not quite disguise. "This is not Europe, my dear. There are so many of them and so few of us. I have heard that you do not approve of our methods in England." I admitted that our government was now determined to abolish slavery in its dominions and was attempting to persuade other countries to follow suit. This plan, so far, has not been entirely successful. There was much laughter from the Portuguese present, while the slaves looked on in silence.

When the carriage arrived to collect me the family also left the house in procession, Dona Gabriela's husband leading, followed by his wife and the older children, with a long string of black slaves following them, nursemaids and bearers, all dressed in the height of Portuguese fashion.

CHAPTER
FOUR

January 6th, 1818

My Dearest Selena,

It will be many months before this letter reaches you but the writing of it eases my mind, and I hope you will be greatly diverted by my account of life at this strange court. I have pursued my duties as lady-in-waiting extraordinaire to Dona Leopoldina for two months as of this week, not counting the long days en-route. My position remains a difficult one and I am not accepted by the Austrian faction, although the princess herself is most gracious to me.

A slave rings a bell in the corridor outside my apartment to summon me to my duties. How I hate this! Only servants are summoned by bells and I am treated as a superior version of one. Yesterday I received my first quarterly payment. An official came and formally handed me a number of gold cruzados, each worth four hundred milreis — about fifty pounds I believe, in a blue velvet bag embroidered with the royal crest in gold thread. Nevertheless, I cannot abide these customs. Only servants and women of the night are paid in this way.

My unfortunate mistress is also finding things difficult here. I think she is already disillusioned with her marriage and she suffers greatly from the heat and the boredom of life at court. She adopts a cheerful pose that is more depressing than outright despair. She now rides out occasionally with Dom Pedro in the countryside adjacent to Rio, but I do not think she is happy with him.

I was presented to the queen when she visited her daughter-in-law's apartments. As I made my courtesy to Queen Carlota, she showed me her full, twisted countenance for a long moment.

"*Qui?*" was her only remark.

"My new lady," replied Dona Leopoldina. "She is from England." Dona Carlota looked me over and I was positively gorgonised by her stare. Her dress was gay and colourful with gold and silver silk embroidery. It was very grand but more suited to a young girl. Her ladies wore equally eccentric garments and I have heard that they sit on the floor oriental-style in their mistress' chambers.

"I do not care for the English, they are a deceitful people." This was Queen Carlota's parting remark as she took her leave. It was made in French but I caught the general drift.

Adelaide has warmed somewhat towards Eufrasia and has undertaken to teach her some English. The slave girl now has a smattering of cockney phrases overlaid with a disconcerting Afro-Brazilian accent. "My eye in a bandbox," one of Adelaide's favourite sayings, is pronounced as "mi eye in a bumbosh." This, combined with the aggravations of royal service, can bring on an attack of the vapours during a humid afternoon. The period after luncheon can only be tolerated if one lies down under a large fan, wearing as little as possible. How shocked everyone at home would be if they could see us!

My friend, Mr Luccombe, has brought me a parcel of goods newly arrived on the packet boat from England. I was delighted to find a new novel I had ordered, Thomas Moore's *Lallah Rookh*. It is an oriental fantasy and I am longing to read it. Moore is an Irishman and a friend of dear Lord Byron. The book has been much praised.

When I read an English novel I am immediately transported back to my home country for a few hours. In the meantime, life here is lived purely for pleasure on the backs of a myriad of slaves and courtiers. I wonder if there is anyone left in Lisbon: the entire population of that city appears to have landed in Rio. Europe, however, is always in our thoughts. All talk is of the latest fashions from Paris, the choicest goods from London, who is being lionised in the theatres and the scandal from the royal courts.

Often, the fashions are completely passé when they arrive here and after they are given an Afro-Brazilian garnish (much beading and feathers), they often appear very strange indeed. We would shock the stately residents of Bath if we appeared on their streets in this finery. They would surely choke on their chocolate.

How I long to receive a letter from you, dear friend! I trust you and dear Miles are well and in the best of spirits and that the gods of fortune are smiling upon you. It seems so long ago since we were all together in London, giving card parties and having adventures in Brighton and Bath, not to mention my experiences in Paris and Venice.

If my relatives could see me now, how amazed they would be, especially my esteemed brother-in-law, Mr Darcy.

But I fear I have been cast off by my family. Who knows when I shall see you all again or set foot on English soil once more? However, I must not give way to a fit of the dismals. I must return to my duties and also do battle with the wildlife. The mosquitoes are outrageous.

With fondest love,

I remain your friend Lydia Wickham

After sealing the letter I made my way to Dona Leopoldina's apartments for our appointed hour of English conversation. On the way I stopped and looked out of a window, where I caught sight of Dom Pedro in the gardens. He was wearing a shining white military tunic adorned with a great deal of gilt frogging. His tight, white breeches were tucked into highly polished black boots. He was idly tickling the rump of a pretty slave girl with his riding crop, as she bent over a spade and turned the earth.

When he caught sight of me, his swarthy face broke into a wide smile and he saluted me with the crop, placing his hand on his heart. I bobbed a curtsy and he blew me a kiss. I moved on hastily but not before His Highness finished this romantic little scene by spitting into the bushes with some expertise. Expectorating contests are held frequently in the gardens, with Dom Pedro competing with guards and servants.

"My husband has an earthy nature," Dona Leopoldina commented on one such occasion. "It must be the Latin temperament," she added without conviction. Indeed, the prince is much pre-occupied

35

with bodily fluids of all kinds and makes no secret of the fact.

I am perturbed by Dom Pedro's interest in me. I fear he has marked me for his next conquest. An Englishwoman at this court is a great novelty and I am regarded as something rich and strange, like a human version of the white tiger, rare and decidedly peculiar. As such, I am a challenge to someone like Dom Pedro.

When my duties were concluded I returned to my rooms, where I found that Adelaide had admitted Jerry Sartain, who was sprawled in a chair looking perfectly at home. I could not imagine how he had gained entry to the palace. The guards must have been asleep at their posts.

"He just turned up like a bad penny," Adelaide explained as Eufrasia came in with coffee. They both departed the room, leaving me alone with Jerry.

"You should teach that girl some English," Jerry remarked, referring to Eufrasia. "How old is she? Her figure is excellent."

"Please do not annoy me with your coarseness," I begged. "Why have you arrived in this manner? I have not seen you since we disembarked from that dreadful ship." Jerry waved away my complaints. "I have had plans to make, my sweet. I am joining an expedition into the interior. Who knows what we may find? I hope to improve my fortunes considerably." He gave me a shrewd look. "I trust you will find ways to do the same." When he saw my expression of concern he stood up and drew me close. "Don't worry about me, Lydia. Think only of yourself. We may meet again one day and, in the meantime, perhaps a last . . .?" He gazed meaningfully at the chaise longue and held me tighter.

"No! No!" I shrieked. "Do not be ridiculous. We are in the royal palace. You should not be here and we cannot afford to be seen together." I noticed that my cries had not brought either of my attendants to my rescue.

My erstwhile admirer shrugged and indicated an oddly shaped container covered with a cloth. "I brought you a farewell gift, sweet Lydia. It will remind you of me every day." I gazed at the object with trepidation as he whipped off the cover. There was an ear-shredding cry as a brilliantly plumaged bird was revealed beating its wings against a cage. I stared at it for a moment, stupefied. Adelaide came into the room, saw the creature and screamed. The large red and green bird screamed back at her. When I turned around I found that Jerry had slipped silently away and I instantly regretted my hasty words as I remembered our delightful coupling so long ago.

The parrot or macaw, or whatever it is, has a rich vocabulary in several languages, eclipsing even the parrot kept by our ship's captain. Only by covering its cage with a cloth can we silence its filthy verbiage. Adelaide has officially named the bird Napoleon but when she thinks I am not present she refers to it as Jerry.

CHAPTER
FIVE

February 3rd

"What do you do with yourself all day, my dear?" Mr Luccombe is filled with curiosity about my role.

"I wait upon Dona Leopoldina, but of course I share the duties with other ladies so I am not required at all hours."

My host's expression became thoughtful and he eyed me keenly. Taking my arm he led me into his study where he picked up a ledger and clutched it to his chest in a solemn manner.

"You must know, my dear, that I am not merely a business man. I also serve my country in various ways. Occasionally, I solicit suitable people to assist me."

The hairs on my arms were standing up at this point, despite the heat. Scenes from my past life flashed before me, the resolute pursuit of my person by Captain Marshfield through various parts of the continent, and his insistence that I spy on the count and the Princess of Wales. No doubt the captain had contacted Mr Luccombe and alerted him to my arrival. I would never be free of the wretch, *and* he still owed me payment. Mr Luccombe's next words confirmed my fears.

"I believe you have served in a certain capacity before, Mrs Wickham. Is that not so?"

Reluctantly, I agreed. "Whatever do you wish me to do here in Brazil?"

"Simply to let us know the mind of Dom Pedro and the royal family. Our government wishes to know their attitude to us. We are, you know, Portugal's oldest ally. That should be worth something." I doubted that the British Government would want to know what was going on in Dom Pedro's mind — I could hazard a guess.

"I should think my services would be worth something also, sir. Yet I have still not been paid for my work in Italy," I replied, a sour note entering my voice.

Mr Luccombe waved the ledger at me, almost dropping it. "Do not concern yourself, my dear. I will reimburse you for your work here."

I sighed, wondering why I was always required to spy on my lovers. I devoutly wished to be with Jerry Sartain at that moment, but even he needed me to obtain money for him. All men require something from us. I sighed again and agreed to Mr Luccombe's proposition.

"Capital! Then you must come with us to watch a procession tomorrow." There is a procession of some kind almost every day in this city. Endless saints' days and national events are commemorated with everyone working themselves into a frenzy. It is quite tiresome, as if London was celebrating a coronation several times each week. Of course, the citizens have so much leisure because all the work is done by slaves.

Seeing my hesitation, Mr Luccombe assured me that tomorrow would be special. "It is the Goldsmiths' procession, the biggest and most popular of them all. Everyone will be out on the street in their finery and there will be a grand firework display afterwards. You must not miss it." No doubt there was an ulterior motive in all of this.

On the following morning Adelaide and I donned our mantillas, anticipating much drunkenness on the streets, intense heat and crowds. I have become quite fond of this headdress but my maid complains that it makes her feel ridiculous.

"We will blend into the crowd with ease if we wear these things," I told her. She disagreed saying, "With our complexions we will stand out like a pimple on a baby's bottom. It's all very well for these girls with their dark, flashing eyes but it doesn't suit an English miss."

When we joined the Luccombes, with their family and slaves, the procession was approaching. The religious emblems and statues borne aloft on great biers were preceded by a strange sight — black women called *Baianas*, from the province of Bahia, were dancing along dressed in the skimpiest of costumes with feathered headdresses. In between the hymns and the devout exclamations, these females were being ogled and cheered as they undulated and shook their bodies in a most suggestive manner.

Everyone followed them from street to street. "Here come the Bananas again," Adelaide called as she ran ahead.

"*Baianas, Baianas*, not bananas," puffed Mr Luccombe, struggling along in his black serge frock coat. In the Street of the Goldsmiths, the sun glinted on gold and silver plaques as the crowd applauded the women again. They were followed by a troupe depicting the sacrifice of Abraham.

"Stop, stop," begged Mrs Luccombe. "Let us fortify ourselves before we go any further."

We stopped to take tiny bowls of black bean broth "to line the stomach" said her husband. These were followed by small glasses of *cachaça*, the local cane sugar spirit, which is a powerful brew. I was quite overcome after one glass and my mantilla fell askew. We all headed towards the parade ground where the fireworks would be held, fighting our way through the heaving crowds. The slaves carried plates and baskets of food, but at that point I gave up the struggle and allowed myself to be borne along by the tide of people.

Suddenly, I was thrust against the chest of a somewhat ruffian-looking fusilier officer who was leaning against the door of a carriage. To my surprise and horror it was Dom Pedro. "Your Highness!" I exclaimed, removing my face from his jacket. "You are . . . here?" I realised how silly the remark sounded but I was taken aback. There was nothing unusual about finding the prince in disguise on the streets of Rio. It was well known that this was his favourite occupation. He found it an invaluable way to meet new female acquaintances.

"How delightful, Meez Wickham!" He flashed a smile full of teeth and pressed me against his chest for a second before releasing me and making a formal bow. "Allow me to escort you, *senhora*."

"To where, Your Highness?" The prince's thick, dark eyebrows shot up like a pair of acrobatic moles over his hot eyes. I had given him an opportunity.

"Let me show you this city — the real Rio de Janeiro. You will be amazed." Whatever he wanted to show me I doubted it would include a great deal of scenery.

"With respect, sire, I must return to the palace to attend on Dona Leopoldina shortly." He waved away this remark, lifted me bodily aside from the *melée* and deposited me in the carriage. I am not averse to assertive behaviour in men, but as we drove away I had a strong feeling that this particular escapade would not end well.

"You have been cold towards me," Dom Pedro crooned in my ear. "Come here you saucy rabbit!" He lunged forward as the carriage swung around a corner.

"But, sire," I protested, to no avail.

"You arouse dark passions in my breast," he continued before lapsing into a mixture of Portuguese and French, apparently exhausted by the effort of speaking a few English sentences. I was not greatly diverted.

We drove fast into the hills towards the Botanical Gardens. My lace mantilla was thrown into a corner of the carriage and the elegant cut work border on my lemon coloured gown was badly crumpled. We stopped among the giant trees in the gardens and tumbled out into the dazzling afternoon.

"We will have a *peekneek*," announced Dom Pedro as he commanded servants to lay out covers and cushions in the place where our bucolic revels would take place. I settled myself down with a wary eye out for the teeming, chirruping wildlife.

My royal admirer waved away his retainers and they settled themselves on the other side of the carriage, making a barrier between us.

"Now we are alone," the prince whispered unnecessarily. The scene was an extraordinary one. I experienced a sense of *deja vu*. How many times had I been in this situation? I tried to collect my wits, knowing that it was important to keep the prince engaged in conversation, but the language problem made this difficult. A vision of Queen Carlota's twisted countenance swam before my eyes.

"Your Highness," I said in my best Portuguese, "I fear your mother would not approve of this tryst." The prince laid his head on my shoulder in a winsome manner.

"My mother is a *beetch*," he declared in English. I was at a loss.

"Dona Leopoldina ..." I began, a note of desperation creeping into my voice.

"She is not here," he replied with relentless logic. Dom Pedro sat up and began to pour liberal glasses of port. We sat in silence propping each other up for a while and after a few glasses of this fortified wine we were overcome by heat and fumes and fell asleep.

When I awoke, the prince's head was again resting on my shoulder and a slave was fanning us with a giant palm leaf. My head and shoulders ached and I felt very thirsty.

After wriggling away from Dom Pedro, I signalled to the servants to convey their master to the carriage and return to the palace. He snored gently all the way home and I slipped back to my apartment unobserved. No doubt he would manage things better at our next meeting.

A messenger was waiting to inform me that Adelaide and the Luccombes were still anxiously scouring the city for me and if I returned in the meantime I should send word to them. I instructed the messenger to escort Adelaide back and to apologise to my hosts saying that I had lost them in the crowd and returned home alone.

Eufrasia brought me lemonade and I retired to rest. Anxious thoughts merged into disagreeable dreams as I wondered what would happen if Dona Leopoldina became aware of her husband's interest in me — not to mention the Countess of K.

The goblin that controls my destiny had been active, I discovered. Unknown to me, I was observed descending from Dom Pedro's carriage by one of the palace servants who spied for Queen Carlota. Although the queen does not live at the palace, preferring her house in Botafogo, she maintains an army of informers to keep her abreast of the goings on at her husband's court.

Adelaide warned me that the servants were abuzz with the news and I was eventually summoned to the queens' presence where she accused me of bringing her son into "disrepute." This was so obviously absurd that

I do not know how I was able to keep from laughing aloud.

"Nothing disreputable occurred, your majesty, I swear," I assured her. The queen waved me away with another muttered remark about the perfidious English. When I returned to my apartment Adelaide exclaimed about how "it doesn't do to become entangled with married men. Remember what happened with the count, madam."

"I do not need any reminders, Adelaide," I replied. "I also recall your adventures with the baker and his wife when we were in Venice." She went off muttering prophecies of doom and later I heard her warbling a bawdy verse called "*The Virgin's Last Resolve.*"

I retired to bed that night in very low spirits, watching from my window a moon so bright it seemed positively indecent. The night air lay around me, heavy and thick like brown velvet.

February 10th

Preparations have been concluded for the long-delayed coronation of Dom João.

He could not be crowned officially until the priests were sure that the soul of his mother, Queen Maria, had left purgatory. I began to understand this attitude despite my Anglican upbringing. Brazil, in all its murderous, insect-ridden beauty was proving to be purgatorial for me and I had so far not received one diamond as consolation.

I did not have long to wait for the goblin of doom to be active once more. A few days later I received a note from Dom Pedro inviting me to visit the markets with him, "To see the city in the raw." The unmarked carriage arrived to convey me to the meeting place. There was no way I could refuse this offer. The prince's word is law and his every whim is indulged. The king is becoming more and more reclusive, spending his time at his country residence, and Dona Leopoldina is pregnant, largely immobile, and quite depressed. Dom Pedro holds centre stage and obviously I was to be his next conquest. Queen Carlota stood poised in the wings to make trouble for everyone, especially for me.

"You should ask for some of them diamonds, madam," Adelaide advised. "At least you will have something to show for your trouble."

I pondered on my royal encounters as I drove to the meeting place. My brief time with the Prince Regent had been fraught with danger, thanks to Jerry Sartain. Dom Pedro would be an improvement in most respects. If I was destined to be a mistress rather than a wife at least I would be a *royal* mistress. I invoked the spirit of Nell Gwyn as I drove on.

Dom Pedro greeted me, again dressed as an ordinary soldier.

We walked in the markets where they sell everything from sugar to slaves to fruit and exotic birds and beasts of all kinds. My heart was almost broken when I heard a beautiful black and yellow bird, a type of oriole called a *sofrê*, singing a sad, tender song as it beat its wings against a cage. I paid to have it released. When we returned to the palace Dom Pedro said, "I will come to your apartment later, *chérie*." In the circumstances, I could only agree.

As I waited for the prince I thought I heard the *sofrê* singing its plaintive tune, so different from Napoleon's squawking and cursing. The prince found the bird amusing. He threatened to bring me an orange-gold tamarin monkey as an extra pet — "A companion for Napoleon." Everything is a great joke to him. "There is a bald-headed, red-faced monkey here. We have named it *macaco Inglês* — English monkey!" I was not amused.

Some rudiments of good sense and propriety came to my aid and I resolved to refuse Dom Pedro's attentions once again. To my surprise he received my refusal in good part.

"I have not sought your good opinion, sire, and I do not deserve it," I assured him.

"But you have it, *chérie*," he replied. "Do not concern yourself." He leaned towards me and I reared back, forcing him to clutch a handful of my gown. I froze for fear of hearing a rending sound. How could I appear before Dona Leopoldina in a torn gown?

Dom Pedro released me and waved a hand nonchalantly. "Shall we take coffee?" He led me outside to his unofficial receiving room, the unmarked carriage. He handed me in and we drove off in sight of numerous attendants.

The prince produced silver-topped containers and poured tiny cups of coffee. I noted that he did not spill a drop after so many years of practice. The tiny cup wobbled as I raised it to my lips. I took a sip and tried to appeal to the higher moral nature that I feared he did not possess. "I am now totally compromised, your highness," I said, with no attempt to disguise the reproach in my voice.

"Do not fear anything, Meez Wickham. You are under my protection and I am the most powerful man in the kingdom — almost." He recollected his reclusive father for a moment.

I was treated to another toothy smile as he produced a box from under a seat. "I have a gift for you, *chérie*. I hope it will amuse you." From its shape I could see that it could not possibly contain any exotic birds. Another parrot would have been beyond intolerable.

The box contained an ivory and ostrich feather fan, painted on one side with a view of Guanabara Bay and the Sugar Loaf and on the other with a message from the prince — and signed by him. He said it was a quotation from a famous Portuguese poet. Naturally, I could not appear in public with this item.

We drove around for a while and he confided in me. I was made privy to his feelings of frustration and resentment about his status. Exiled from Portugal, "That poor little country," as he called it, he dreams of ruling the vast lands of Brazil, "A country worthy of an Emperor." I suppose all heirs in waiting feel this way. Unlike his mother, who hates Brazil, Dom Pedro loves his tropical realm. His father, the king, also loves the place. I wonder if deep down they realise they will have to return home one day. I would have to relay all this information to Mr Luccombe later.

48

As we drove, he produced roasted grasshopper from his pocket which he relishes as a snack. He tried to tempt me with this delicacy but I declined. "They taste like hazelnuts and have the consistency of shrimp," he explained. Shrimp, shrimp paste, manioc meal, black beans and rice, how happy I will be never to eat these things again. When we returned to the palace, Dom Pedro bade me a fond farewell assuring me of his devotion and his speedy return. I made a deep curtsy as he departed.

I had not thought the prince capable of playing a waiting game, but he continues to seek my company and woo me with little gifts. I am now the talk of the court, but if Dona Leopoldina has heard anything she ignores it. Her attitude towards me remains unchanged.

CHAPTER
SIX

February 16th

A few days later, Adelaide handed me a letter from Dom Pedro in which he informed me that he had commissioned an artist to undertake a secret assignment and that I should be ready to pose for this artist in a day or two. Immediately, I fell into a state of great excitement at the prospect of having my likeness painted. I would be immortalised.

"Adelaide," I commanded, "you must make a cull of my gowns, reserving only the best. I will select some jewellery." I would need to have my hair washed, curled and enhanced. The following day passed in a happy contemplation of my appearance and how I would appear to posterity. I wondered, in passing, why I was not to sit for the artist in his studio, but no doubt he would explain matters.

In the event my anticipation was a little premature. At lunchtime I found Adelaide unwell after agreeing to partake of a meal consisting of beef, rice and pumpkin with toasted manioc, accompanied by a terrifyingly hot chili sauce. She lay gasping on her bed, occasionally burying her face and lolling tongue completely in a bowl of water. She was *hors de combat* for a good three quarters of an hour and I was obliged to have tea served by Eufrasia, who never manages to brew it to my taste. I closed my eyes and imagined myself drinking orange pekoe at Longbourn, with a light English drizzle falling gently outside.

When my maid recovered the power of speech she accused Eufrasia of tricking her into eating the food, calling her "a black devil". The slave girl quickly disappeared from view after throwing murderous glances at Adelaide. Now I am bedevilled with servant problems in my hour of need. In truth, I was alarmed at Adelaide's suffering but she has recovered quite well, although still not able to assist me with my toilette.

I summoned Eufrasia and berated her sharply. "You cannot behave to my maid in that manner," I told her. "Remember your place, my girl. I have treated you well and I do not expect to be served so ill." Adelaide tottered in at that moment urging me in a hoarse voice to "sell the wench in the slave market." I could not do such a cruel thing but Eufrasia bared her teeth in a sinister manner and scuttled away like a rat with a chicken bone. I was quite discombobulated for a moment but I returned quickly to the problem of preparing myself for the portrait as a monumental effort was required. I instructed my maid to give directions as I attempted to arrange myself. Unfortunately, her voice disappeared after a few minutes and she resorted to miming directions.

Dom Pedro arrived with the artist to find me curled and adorned to perfection (or close to it) in sea green silk and white lace. The prince appeared not to notice my finery saying that he had commissioned lovers' eyes, the miniature portraits popularised by the Prince Regent. As always, he was aware of English fashion.

"You will wear a tiny portrait of my brown eye, chérie, and I will wear your beautiful blue eye." So much for my gowns and hairstyle.

The matter was concluded quickly. The artist made a sketch of my eye which would be painted on to a tiny piece of ivory. He took Dom Pedro's likeness in the same way and as he was preparing to depart, the door of my chamber was flung open and a royal servant announced Dona Leopoldina.

We all froze, as far as anyone can do such a thing in this climate. The artist shielded his face with his sketchbook as if this action would render him invisible. I found that I had been holding my breath for several seconds and it expired with a gasp. Dom Pedro remained nonchalant, as always. He advanced on his wife and attempted to embrace her but could not encompass her bulk. She spat a sentence in German which sounded most uncomplimentary, so it is as well that he does not understand the language.

My mistress spied the fan lying on a table and seized it, examining the writing and growing scarlet in the face with fury. She turned to me, exclaiming in English, "So this is how you betray me!" I was overcome with mortification, dear reader. My knowledge of Portuguese was not good enough to translate the verse on the fan. I had accepted the prince's explanation of it — unwisely, as it turned out.

Several members of the court crowded around Dona Leopoldina, reading the fan and exclaiming. Contemptuous looks were cast in my direction. It appeared that the verse was a salacious one taken from what Dona Leopoldina described as a "filthy *modinho*" — one of the popular songs current in Rio. In short, I was summarily dismissed from her service and told not to darken her presence again. As she swept out her husband murmured, "Do not upset yourself, my love." For a moment I thought he was addressing me.

When I was alone again — the artist having left with the crowd, followed by the prince, I sank down on a couch in despair, throwing the fan on the floor in disgust. "What am I to do?" I wailed. It was so unjust: after all, I had not even graced the prince's bed.

I was at a loss to know where all this would lead. I recalled my unfortunate liaison with the Austrian Count and the episode with the Prince Regent. Close encounters with royalty had not benefited me greatly. Either a title or a number of diamonds might compensate me for an enforced stay in the tropics and a dalliance with Brazil's swarthy Prince Charming. How could I present this argument to Dom Pedro in a tactful manner? In the event, I did not have the opportunity as I was kept in enforced idleness in my apartment, forbidden to venture near my mistress. Knowing I now had nothing to lose, I made no resistance when the prince returned to my apartment intent on seduction.

While Eufrasia spread my bed with pristine embroidered French linen, he told me that he planned to take a river journey into the interior on the royal yacht and that I was to accompany him. "We will have fun, *chérie*." I smiled sweetly, at a loss to know how to reply to this.

As we lay together, I looked up at the blue silk hangings I had purchased to make my bed appear more regal. Although Dom Pedro was too swarthy to be described as handsome he was certainly an improvement on the Prince Regent in looks. As a lover, he was energetic and considerate and if I replaced his face with Lord Byron's in my mind, who was to know? After our lovemaking Eufrasia served our guest with a banana *compôte* which he ate with great enjoyment. Bananas in every form are adored here.

Before we left on the voyage I paid a visit to my friends, the Luccombes, to tell them the news. I can be perfectly frank with them without fear of reproach. Mrs Luccombe clucked and sympathised for a moment, then began complaining that her servants were "encroaching", as she put it. "The slaves must be watched like hawks," she assured me.

"And then there are the tradespeople here and the Portuguese officials who are either out to rob you or are too unconscionably idle to execute any task," she added.

"It is the heat," her husband murmured before settling back in his chair and nodding off. Mrs Luccombe and I continued to sit in companionable silence on the veranda, rocking gently and fanning ourselves. It was a peaceful if not very merryfiying afternoon, but I had escaped from the palace for a few hours.

Mr Luccombe woke with a start at one point and asked me how often I had to kiss the king's hand. He chuckled over this before nodding off again and I realised that I would never need to kiss the king's hand again now that I was a pariah. As I sat quietly, I could see a flock of exquisite humming birds in the trees. These tiny creatures are called *beija-flor*, flower kissers, by the locals. Dreamily, I watched through half closed eyes as the tiny creatures darted back and forth. Some were emerald green with copper rumps, others ruby throated or white-capped. As they sipped from the flowers their wings beat at a frantic speed making a distinctive humming sound.

They were graceful, beautifully-coloured and useful. If only I could say the same about myself. For a moment I felt as if I was in Paradise. Gone were the mosquito bites, the smells and bodily discomforts, gone were the annoying Portuguese and Austrian aristocrats, the heat that sapped one's will, the endless shrimp and manioc. I was a dryad flitting between brilliant foliage . . .

I woke with a start as Mrs Luccombe prodded my arm. "Your mouth was open, Lydia dear. You were beginning to drool."

CHAPTER
SEVEN

February 19th

At last! I have a letter from Selena. My dear friend writes at length . . .

Dearest Lydia,

We were delighted to receive a letter from you and to hear that you are well and prospering in that far off country. I am a little worn down by our financial misfortunes but otherwise well. Miles is flourishing, as always, and is full of schemes to improve our lot, sadly without much success.

We have returned from Paris and are now living in a small cot in Stoke Newington. It is beyond dreadful to be so far from town, but my husband has been engaged by a local squire to teach his son the rudiments of fencing, shooting and other martial arts. The small salary offered enables us to live tolerably well. How I miss the days when we held card soirées with you, dear Lydia! We had such fun and filled our coffers admirably.

My news will be very old by the time it reaches you. Do you receive any copies of Ackermann's Repository? The fashions for the coming season involve much frilling on skirts.

Miles took me to London a few weeks ago to see Edmund Kean play *Shylock* at Drury Lane. What a fine performer, a veritable giant of an artiste!

I hope you are not still in contact with that scoundrel of a highwayman, dear Lydia. No good will come of that. Surely you have an unrivalled opportunity to catch an aristocrat at court? Miles asks why you have not snared a duke, as he suggested?

(If only they knew of my situation.)

Do you remember Miles meeting that blue stocking woman in Bath? Mary Shelley is the wife (perhaps) of the notorious poet. It is rumoured that she has written a particularly frightful Gothic novel about a monster which will be published next year. I will certainly send you a copy, knowing your fondness for such things.

The Queen Charlotte is in poor health and not expected to survive the year. The Prince Regent remains unchanged (but fatter). I have heard no news of your family at Pemberley.

Write again and tell us more of your life in Brazil. I remain, dear Lydia, your fondest friend,

Selena Caruthers

February 21st

Today I have received another gift from the prince, a fragrance pendant on a tasselled gold chain. The container is ivory with a cracked gold surface depicting two lovers. The fragrance escapes from holes in the side as it is worn throughout the day.

"Not that you are not fragrant enough, *chérie*," Dom Pedro told me as we boarded the royal yacht to begin our cruise, no doubt, to the chagrin of the entire court. The prince remained unruffled and received me on board with great enthusiasm. As we left the shore, we promenaded on deck while a string quartet played lively airs.

Adelaide had, of course, accompanied me and she lost no time in gathering the gossip below decks.

"He has taken his mistresses on cruises before," she informed me.

"What became of those women?"

"Well, you know about the French ballet dancer?"

"Yes, yes!"

"She was sent away up country when they discovered she was with child."

"And?"

"She died!" I was horrified, I dreaded such a predicament befalling me. I had managed to avoid pregnancy ever since my marriage to Mr Wickham, by various methods. Perhaps I was simply fortunate or possibly infertile. Such a condition would prove expedient for someone in my position.

"There's many a slip," said Adelaide, reading my thoughts, as always.

The voyage proceeded well enough, thank heaven. It lasted for only two weeks and we remained close to the river bank which was greatly to be preferred to the terrors of the high seas. We retired to Dom Pedro's luxuriously appointed quarters in the heat of the afternoon for an hour of dalliance and a long siesta.

Occasionally, the ship halted at remote settlements where the local residents came to honour the prince. Imagine my astonishment, dear reader, when we docked at an isolated estate surrounded by forest and among those arriving to pay their respects, I spied Jerry Sartain. He was accompanied by a pretty mulatto girl who was introduced as his wife. A bevy of buxom slave girls followed behind. I was astonished, jealous and not a little angry.

"He didn't waste much time," Adelaide commented, voicing my own thoughts. When I beheld the group arrayed in all kinds of exotic finery, I guessed that my highwayman had quickly found his niche, and had acquired enough money to purchase this harem.

I bit my lip in mortification as Jerry smirked at me and bowed low to Dom Pedro, who explained that these men were rubber barons.

"Robber barons more like," I mumbled to myself.

I heard Adelaide mutter something about "He should have hanged at Newgate."

I could not help thinking of what might have been. No man had conquered my heart — or indeed the rest of me, as Jerry had done. What if I had been braver, if we had slipped away together from the palace? Might we have been happy in this tropical forest miles from any society, or would he have tired of me? These thoughts ran swiftly through my head as Jerry kissed my hand.

"How delightful to meet a fellow countrywoman!" he exclaimed as Dom Pedro beamed at us. We were invited to drink coffee at the estate house where Jerry appeared to be in charge. Everything became clear when he explained that his bride, Consuela, was the daughter of a local rubber baron known as "The Colonel." They are all called colonel, these leaders of parties of brigands. They are marauding freebooters who exploit the rich resources and oppress the natives. No doubt, Jerry had made himself indispensable.

When we were unobserved I whispered to him, "How could you . . . you traitor!"

He raised his eyebrows and replied, "All's fair in love and war, my dear."

"You gave me nothing but a parrot," I whispered, "and you took all my money." He shrugged and smiled the charming, lopsided smile that disarms everyone.

"You have managed to snare a prince, my dear. You can't complain." I sniffed, feeling close to tears.

"You know I care for you."

At this point, I noticed that Dom Pedro had walked back to the riverbank and was unbuttoning his britches, in the company of his attendants, before urinating into the sluggish water. I sighed and turned away.

As we returned to the ship and the party on shore doffed their hats enthusiastically, I wondered again if our paths might cross in the future, Jerry's and mine. I stood at the rail full of regret and nostalgia as the figures disappeared from view.

Adelaide said, "That one always turns up sooner or later. Born to hang, if you ask me."

"I did not ask you," I snapped and went to have lunch with the prince. The sight of more shrimp in this heat made me feel distinctly queasy. I pecked at something called *escondidinho* — something hidden. This dish consists of dried shrimp covered with a purée of mashed manioc and grated cheese. One is obliged to cut a hole in the crust to fish out the shrimp. A great deal of effort for very little reward.

Dom Pedro attacked the dish with enthusiasm, his eyebrows becoming even more active than usual.

"I have told the chef to serve us a risotto of *pitangas* for dinner," he said.

"*Pitangas?*"

He nodded. "They are delicious, tiny rain forest berries served with—"

"Let me guess," I cried. "Shrimp!"

"Giant shrimps!" He beamed.

I eventually received the prince's miniature just after we returned from the cruise. It was no more than two inches long and set in a gold bangle with a few pearls and sapphires. My own eye was set in an oval frame surrounded by seed pearls and worn on a fob watch.

"No diamonds then, madam?" Adelaide remarked unnecessarily.

It was a charming gesture of the prince's regard and affection for me. I had no illusions that true love entered into the mix. How I would have loved an elegant, full length portrait in oils fine enough to grace the wall of an ancestral pile. However, as I did not have the latter, it was as well that I did not have the former.

Adelaide speculated on how much the infamous fan would fetch in one of London's "flash houses." "It's a pity the words are in Portuguese. The locals in Shoreditch wouldn't get the joke."

CHAPTER
EIGHT

As the yacht made its way back to Rio, I ventured to ask Dom Pedro about my position at the court.

"Surely I cannot stay at the palace now that I am no longer part of Dona Leopoldina's entourage? I am shunned by everyone." Dom Pedro scratched his sideburns and thought for a moment.

"I shall find a house for you — somewhere up in the hills above the city. You will find it most attractive." And lonely, I thought. "Perhaps not in Botofago," the prince added, "that would be too near my mother." I reminded him again that I would have little company. Nobody from the court would visit me. "Let them eat shit!" was his characteristic reply, not a remark that offered much consolation.

And so we were on the move once more. Adelaide packed our belongings assisted by Eufrasia. There is now an uneasy truce between them, but the slave girl would accompany us to the new house. "She can carry the bird," Adelaide told me.

It was a melancholy departure: no one at court came to bid me farewell. I had made no friends there and if anyone had nursed cordial feelings towards me, Dona Leopoldina's disapproval would have inhibited them.

After our few belongings were transported away we left in the inevitable unmarked carriage. I had already received my final bag of gold coins from a court official. As we travelled through the streets of Rio, admiring the vista of the great bay, I cooled myself with the fan that I could not help regarding as the cause of all my troubles.

We settled ourselves into the house well enough. It has fine views over the bay, but as I predicted we are very much alone. The Luccombes loyally came to call. I believe they are genuinely fond of me but, of course, Mr Luccombe needed a report from me. Dom Pedro will visit but otherwise I will have ample leisure to enjoy the view of the Sugar Loaf Mountain and its environs.

March 10th

A feeling of lassitude and a general weariness with daily life has overwhelmed me of late, quite unlike my usual high spirited self. The sight and smell of shrimp and certain other foods has become distasteful to me. Adelaide has been eyeing me in a speculative fashion and the reason for my symptoms is now apparent. I can no longer keep down my food.

"I believe I am being poisoned!" I cried. "Is it by order of Queen Carlota or has Eufrasia been putting charms in the food?"

"My eye in a bandbox," Adelaide declared. "You are in the family way, madam, if I am not much mistaken."

"No!" I moaned, after resuming an upright position. "It cannot be. It has never happened before."

"There's a first time for everything," my maid replied. "You have just been lucky before, madam."

Luck, *buon fortuna* . . . when had such a thing ever dogged my footsteps? All my plans have come to naught. I have been betrayed by every man I became involved with — and now this — the greatest misfortune that can befall a woman. The news must be broken to Dom Pedro and I do not know how he will react. I remembered the unfortunate French ballerina and shuddered.

I had fully expected to die of some unspeakable disease while in the tropics but the thought of giving birth in this dangerous hothouse was unendurable. Dismal thoughts chased around in my head until I became nauseous once more. Eufrasia stood by, expressionless as always.

"I can make a herbal remedy to help you, madam." She went off to the kitchen followed by Adelaide, "to see that she doesn't get up to any witchcraft." Whatever the ingredients were, they had a soothing effect and I was able to rest while I awaited the arrival of the prince.

Dom Pedro was all concern when I broke the news to him. He was, after all, quite accustomed to such crises. He assured me that all my needs would be met and the best possible care lavished upon me. There was a pause, then he added. "You will not, however, be able to remain in Rio, my love. We must avoid an open scandal and you will need to await the birth somewhere outside the city." I almost laughed aloud. Scandal? Avoidance! When had the prince ever concerned himself with such things? He must be afraid of the

Church. Perhaps the Archbishop will report him to the Vatican. "Let me think about it and I will arrange something." He gave me a quick peck on the cheek and departed while I called for more herbal tea.

March 15th

Within a few days arrangements were made. My belongings were packed once again and Dom Pedro waxed lyrical about my destination as we ate a farewell dinner. At least, the prince ate heartily while I nibbled on a crust. I have scarcely eaten a thing for weeks and I am slowly fading away.

My destination is to be a small town by the sea some hours west of Rio. It is called Paraty. As the prince described it to me, I knew that Adelaide and Eufrasia were listening out on the veranda.

"You will love it there," Dom Pedro assured me. "Drinking passion fruit liqueur by an indigo sea in Paraty, you will think you are in Paradise. I have arranged guards and a chaperone for you. The Count of Paraty will know of your arrival." There was nothing more to discuss. It was necessary to remove me as soon as possible. I had been arranged, tidied and disposed of — for a while, at least. No mention was made of my return to Rio and what would happen to our relationship but I had a conviction that it would be over. The prince would look for new amours, although he has promised that the child will be given a suitable title and status.

I recalled that the bastard offspring of Charles II and Nell Gwyn had been made dukes and earls and that half the English aristocracy was descended from that union. I day-dreamed of something similar for our child. I would be the mother of a noble even if not one myself. When I told Adelaide of this, she made one of her sharp comments about the best laid plans, etc.

March 20th

Today the Countess of K informed me by letter, with great relish, that Dona Leopoldina did not wish me to wait upon her to make my farewells. She has been told of the situation and I admit that I would not wish to meet her face to face at this time. Instead I am to be introduced to my chaperone, my duenna, my dragon lady companion.

Dona Serafina is a tightly wound column of black clad righteousness, bone thin, with an equally thin, aristocratic face. She is long in nose, hair and reproaches. I think she finds her allotted task as unpleasant as I find her company. The only blessing is that her English is minimal, so Adelaide and I can speak freely. A midwife will follow us to Paraty in a few months. I made a farewell visit to the Luccombes, who commiserated with me and refrained from judgement. I doubt I will be sending any interesting reports from my hideaway.

Dom Pedro is eloquent on the subject of Paraty and its attractions.

"The explorer, Amerigo Vespucci, declared that if there is a paradise on earth it must be in that place." He assured me that a charming and appropriate house had been prepared for me and all would be well. I was not to concern myself. A quick kiss and then he was gone. I sat nonplussed amid our packed trunks as Dona Serafina descended from a carriage with her baggage. Eufrasia offered tea to the dragon lady, who settled herself in a chair and began ostentatiously telling her rosary beads. She conveys without words her distaste at having to provide a façade of respectability to someone who does not deserve it.

Tomorrow we leave for Paraty by ship — the little town is not accessible by road, except from over the mountains, the route by which the treasure was brought there to be shipped to Portugal in the last century. Now the seemingly endless stream of gold and precious stones has all but dried up and the ships no longer leave from the port.

"Do you think the town will be a kind of tropical Brighton, madam?" Adelaide always looks on the bright side of life. "I do not think it will resemble Brighton in any way," I assured her. "But we can count on the sunshine."

My bodyguard of ten men is headed by a Captain da Silva, a Portuguese soldier of fortune and a man you would not wish to have as your enemy. The men he commands are similarly hardened veterans of long years fighting in the Americas. The captain left his native Coimbra for the New World at the age of sixteen, and he has been in the service of the Braganças for more than a decade.

His skin is weather beaten and mahogany coloured, his legs bowed from much horse riding, and his sword is ever ready. Da Silva has one thing in common with Dona Serafina and the rest of the entourage — he hates this assignment, guarding a lone female in a backwater where very little happens.

March 27th

Dom Pedro kept his word: the house chosen for me is delightful. It stands on a street named after Dona Geralda — a lady I am not acquainted with. Although it is not as large as the manor houses built by the merchants, which are decorated with strange Masonic symbols, it is in the colonial style, filled with dark mahogany and Brazil wood furniture and pretty Portuguese tiles. White lace curtains drift in the warm breeze and even the blue and white paint gleaming in the sun has a self-satisfied look. Pineapple symbols hang from wrought iron fittings on the façade of the house. They are found everywhere here and I am told they are an African symbol of good fortune. The town is very small; Brighton would seem a great metropolis in comparison.

Visitors are rare because I am considered a pariah. The Count of Paraty made an official visit at Dom Pedro's request but his wife refuses to receive me and the matrons of the town have followed suit. As Dom

Pedro's discarded mistress, I have no status but I must be protected for the sake of his unborn child. The next six months will be the longest of my life.

Adelaide suggested that I might try to pen one of the Gothic novels I enjoy so much, but I fear my literary skills are inferior for such a task. The prince does not communicate with me. I do not expect a visit and I know how poor his writing skills are. His education has been sporadic at best and he finds letter writing a great chore.

Perhaps another letter from Selena will find its way to me — even a missive from my family, although I fear they have cast me off. If they knew of my situation they would certainly disown me. I have not told Selena of my plight. I cannot risk discovery by anyone in England.

And so I have reached paradise — or as close to it as I will get in this world or the next, no doubt. How strange that I feel so isolated in the midst of servants and soldiers and chaperones. I am close to no one. Paraty is indeed a paradise — for sloths. Little gets done in this haven by the blue and gold bay under gently waving palms. This suits me for the moment but, in truth, I could not endure it forever.

"I shouldn't think anything has happened in this place since Domesday," is Adelaide's verdict. Captain da Silva disagrees; "On the contrary, the town saw many skirmishes with pirates in the not too distant past."

"You mean when the treasure ships were here?" I replied. "Those days are long gone."

"Not so long gone." He shrugged. "The pirate crews loved this place. They buried their treasure here. It is said they will return." Da Silva likes to make these pronouncements. He seeks to impress the womenfolk. My dragon lady chaperone gave a well-bred snort of derision as the captain walked away.

The men while away their time well enough, drinking *cachaça* — for which the town is famous — and dallying with the mulatto girls who are often dazzlingly beautiful. Sometimes the captain can be seen gazing wistfully out to sea from the Embarcadero, perhaps hoping for an invasion by those pirates so that he can have a good skirmish.

March 30th

It is true, I discovered, that a cache of treasure was unearthed in the past and used to build one of the churches. There is a church for the slaves, another for the mulattos and a third for the white elite.

As for me, I have promenaded around the harbour and up to the ruined fort, viewed the three or four churches and admired the pretty architecture. On the full moon every month the tide washes into the town over the huge uneven cobblestones laid down by slaves. This is the height of excitement in Paraty.

We spend many hours rocking in our chairs on the veranda, having little else to do. There is a garden filled with vivid foliage but we seldom venture there for fear of snakes and other creatures. I have few books to occupy my time although the Luccombes have promised to send packages and letters from time to time. They will keep me informed of the latest scandals at the court and the names of Dom Pedro's latest conquests but I shall have little of interest to send them now that I am away from the court. Mr Luccombe has had my last report. I shall have few opportunities to observe the prince in future, I suspect. Unless the pirates re-appear, there will be nothing to write about.

Now I am perforce required to turn my hand to embroidering clothes for the expected infant, although needlework was never one of my skills.

When night descends, as it does suddenly in this latitude, Captain da Silva loves to regale us with ghastly stories about Brazil's wildlife — the more horrific the better. We sit whiling away the last, magical sunset minutes drinking passion fruit juice and wine, while he warns us that howler monkeys will pelt you with their own excrement if you venture near them.

With a glance at my swelling body he tells us that the female anaconda, the largest snake in these parts, devours her partner when she is pregnant. This caused some titters from Adelaide and I hid a smile.

"There are stories of giant sloths inhabiting the Pantanal," da Silva continued. "The largest of these is a monster that the Indian tribes call a *mapinguari*."

"Have you seen this creature?" I asked.

"No, but I do not doubt its existence. They say it utters dreadful cries." The captain has travelled in the jungles near the great Amazon River, where he has seen all manner of extraordinary creatures. The fantastic flora and fauna, together with the climate of such a place, would be unendurable for me. I would rather spend a century in Meryton. It was not long after this conversation that Adelaide had an experience which I am sure will remain with her for the rest of her life.

CHAPTER
NINE

April 10th

One evening when the tropical sky began to darken rapidly my maid ventured off the veranda into the garden for a few minutes. I suspected her of taking up the vice of smoking small cigarillos which some of the servant class here indulge in. She hotly denied this, but why else would she have been in that place as darkness fell? I do not believe she was seeking a lover's tryst.

My maid claims that she was suddenly attacked or molested by a monstrous creature, "Like something from one of them horror stories you are always reading, madam."

In the dim light, she made out that the creature was covered in reddish hair and had the body of a large dog but the face of a rabbit. It stood upright waving its clawed hands or paws at her while it barked, purred and whistled in a positively operatic manner.

Hearing her screams, I called for the guard. Da Silva and his men rushed out with lit tapers and there was a good deal of laughing and jeering at poor Adelaide's expense. They watched with glee as my maid and the creature danced a frantic jig around each other, while I upbraided the men from the veranda calling them cowards and rogues.

Eventually, they shooed the creature into the bushes and bundled Adelaide into the house where Eufrasia and I were obliged to ply her with brandy. She was still gibbering with fright, claiming to be suffering from the heebie jeebies, when da Silva appeared.

"What was that thing?" I demanded. "Why did you not act immediately?" The captain collapsed into a chair with his sword belt undone. He seized the brandy bottle and took a good slurp.

"It would not have hurt anyone, it was probably terrified of her. The creature is called a capybara. It is a kind of rodent — the largest known, I believe."

"You mean it was a giant rat?"

"It is from the same family."

Adelaide, now recovered, declared that she had been molested by a giant terrier/rabbit cross with a choir boy's voice — "and it had claws!"

Such a perversion of nature is not uncommon in this strange country. We both retired to bed feeling weak and terrified. Should I encounter such a creature in my present condition I shall surely miscarry, or bring forth a monster.

This morning, Adelaide had recourse to some of the herbal remedies she obtained from a Syrian merchant in Rio. "Fear of catastrophe grass" is the remedy, plus holy grass for stomach upsets, "just in case."

Apart from this minor contretemps, life continues in its usual boring manner. I have little to do except contemplate the view, embroider baby clothes and review my various bodily discomforts. As to my future, I scarcely dare think on it. My child will be provided for, but what of its mother?

May 1st

A ship arrived in the bay this morning — a larger ship than we usually see in these parts. The small fishing boats scuttered around it like colourful marine bees. The vessel flies the flag of Texas and I wager it will cause some heartburn in this town.

I sent Adelaide to see what all the fuss was about. A large contingent of local worthies and the count himself came out to meet the captain and his crew, she informed me. Her behaviour has been somewhat strange in the last few hours, especially when she told me that the captain had expressed a wish to call upon me. This, in itself, is such an unusual occurrence that I was quite discombobulated. How does he know of my existence — and what does he want with me?

Soon afterwards, Captain da Silva informed me that the captain and his crew were on their way to the house. The crew is reputed to be armed and da Silva has called the guard to attention outside the building. He has a mad gleam in his eye and I fear a stand-off. He is desperate for some military action.

I recognised the captain immediately when he entered the house; not by sight, because we have never met, but I have seen his likeness often in Rio. His exploits are known all over the Caribbean and the

South Seas. He is Jean Lafitte, notorious pirate and American patriot.

Lafitte looks older than my father ... sixtyish perhaps. He is stocky in build but his black hair and beard are only lightly tinged with grey and his black eyes are fierce and intense. While I was noting these facts, I became aware that my maid was breathing loudly and in a hoarse manner like a rusty walrus. Was she suffering from a sudden attack of bronchial fever?

I followed the direction of her gaze and saw that it was fixed on the El Greco profile of Lafitte's first officer. Although bristling with guns and knives, this man sported a pristine white lace collar like a cavalier. Indeed, with his scarlet jacket, long hair and gleaming sword he could have posed as Prince Rupert of the Rhine, whose portrait hangs in my father's library at home.

Adelaide's breathing was becoming terrifying. The officer gave her a flirtatious wink and I doubt she will be of any use to me for a week. I invited the men to sit and offered them refreshments. They downed glasses of *cachaça* and passion fruit liqueur very rapidly and waved away the sweetmeats. I also subsided gratefully onto a couch arranging my bulk as inconspicuously as possible.

Lafitte greeted me politely but there is an underlying air of menace about him that does not bode well. However, I must remember that I am British, a compatriot of Nelson and Wellington. I gave Adelaide a slap on the back to bring her to her senses and addressed Lafitte boldly.

"You are a long way from home, captain. What can a proud citizen of the United States be doing sailing around Brazilian waters? What can this little town offer you?" Lafitte pulled at his beard and his face darkened as he answered.

"We have been burned out of our base at Barataria by the authorities. I saved New Orleans from the British and all I received in return was a piece of paper. I am now a citizen of the USA but I am penniless. My people are established on a bare island in the Gulf of Texas, near Galveston. What recompense is that?" I detected a slight sneer in his voice when he emphasised the word British and my hackles rose immediately.

"I heard you were also given a pardon for your activities, sir. Is that not worth a great deal?" The captain gave an unpleasant smile in return, assuring me that he came in peace to Paraty and meant no harm to anyone. I could not let that pass.

"I am sure that you are not merely making a social call, captain. You should know that the treasure ships are long gone. This little town is now a peaceful backwater."

Lafitte pulled at his beard again. "I am sixty-eight years old, madam, and I wish to retire in peace. But first I must recoup my losses and for this I must needs travel far afield. There are reports of buried treasure — and other things of value in these parts."

So now he has reached the nub of the matter. I wondered what the Count of Paraty would say about treasure seekers in his territory — and would da Silva's men be any match for Lafitte's crew?

"What will you do if you do not find any treasure?" I enquired. This question elicited more beard pulling. I knew that he had been born on the French island of Saint Domingue and his slight French accent became more pronounced. "Then I will have to consider other opportunities." He eyed me in a speculative manner and I was not greatly diverted.

The men got up to leave after assuring me of their respect for his Portuguese majesty and their gratitude for my "charming company." The cavalier who had such a devastating effect on Adelaide was sprawled on a chair and rose with all his armaments clanking, winking at Adelaide again and making me an extravagant bow. The captain has been sensible enough to bring only a few of his more respectable looking officers with him. I dared not imagine the motley group still on board the ship.

When they had departed, I told Eufrasia to boil a kettle for more herbal tea. I retired to the veranda and as I collected my thoughts I could hear the thrumble of the kettle in the nearby kitchen. I rocked in my chair puzzling as to the reason for the captain's visit. He had not called on anyone else after greeting the count. I was aware of my maid somewhere behind me floating several inches off the ground. Eufrasia appeared and spat neatly over the veranda rail, pointing to her temple.

"That one is *loca*," she assured me. "Now she do no work." She spat again and walked off. Adelaide suddenly found her voice, her breathing almost normal.

"Do you think they will visit us again?"

I nodded, filled with gloom. "I fear that Captain Lafitte has some plans for me and I need to know what they are. I am sure he will be back."

My maid's eyes shot fire. "Of course he will bring his officers with him, won't he?"

I eyed her speculatively. If only I could change places with her, but my bulk prevented this. In addition, my condition meant that I suffered continual uneasiness in the stomach. Adelaide had told me that I was "quite wamblecropt." I am not always sure of her meaning. I could only hope that Lafitte and his pirates would drink too much *cachaça* at a local inn and would be in the same condition for a while.

Indeed, could my position be more parlous? Heavily with child and unable to escape from this place, I could hardly take the donkey trail they called *caminho do ouro* into the mountains. If I left by ship, I had a feeling that it would be on Lafitte's vessel to who knew where? And who would attend to me when I gave birth? I ground my teeth in frustration and one carious tooth gave an explosion of pain. My mother always said that a woman loses a tooth for every child.

Another terrifying thought occurred to me. I called Adelaide back, then decided that she was in no condition to carry out my request so I summoned da Silva instead. He rushed in waving a pistol in an unnecessary manner. "Put that thing away, sir. I need you to bury my jewels now that there are pirates in town!"

CHAPTER
TEN

May 3rd

My jewels — Mrs Makepeace's pearls (a bequest from my former employer), the Prince Regent's necklace (a gift for services rendered), and most of the remaining gold coins in my possession — have been buried in a safe place. Da Silva's men are huddled together in corners while their captain makes plans to attack Lafitte's crew. I shudder to think what will happen. Cunning and careful planning are required, not hot headed encounters.

I have written letters to both Dom Pedro and Mr Luccombe, telling them of our plight. One or other of them, or possibly both, might send help, I am sure. I overruled da Silva's objections and sent one of his most trusted men off to the *Caminho* by night, while Lafitte and his crew were drinking *pinga* in a local tavern. *Pinga* is the popular name for *cachaça*. The messenger will go to the nearest city across the mountains, Ouro Preto, and deliver a message to the governor to send soldiers. Of course, the Count of Paraty should do this, but Portuguese officials do not act quickly. My letters can be sent on to Rio de Janeiro from there.

In the meantime, I am greatly irritated by the behaviour of the females in this house. Dona Serafina moans constantly of her fear of being raped by the pirates, while Adelaide cannot wait to be swept off her feet by the first officer — a Spanish American from New Orleans, we have discovered, who goes by the name of Tom or Tomas Ramirez.

After supervising the burial of my jewels, I tried to distract my mind from the vexatious situation in the usual way — re-reading one of my favourite Gothic novels, Mrs Radcliffe's *A Sicilian Romance*. As I was reading the opening pages, describing a ruined castle set on the shores of a picturesque bay with mountains and forests in the background, I was struck by the similarities between the story and the setting of Paraty. Of course, there is also a small town here but, nevertheless, it could almost be the same place. It occurred to me that I might, after all, turn my hand to writing a Romance. What better distraction could I have in this troublesome situation?

The exotic Brazilian setting might give my story some added spice and originality. Perhaps I could send the manuscript to England with Mr Luccombe's help? Carried away by enthusiasm, I called for pen and paper.

In a flash, a title for my story came to mind. It would be called, *"There Must Be Murder"*. It would incorporate all the requisite features of the Gothic tale: a ruinous castle, a cruel husband and father with a wife imprisoned in a subterranean prison, no doubt. There would be an enquiring heroine who attempts to unravel a ghastly plot at her peril.

I had just determined that my heroine would be called Laurencia, who would be a creature of extreme sensibility and ardent imagination, when I was interrupted by Captain da Silva, who informed me that there was gossip in the town relating to me. I turned to him, demanding to know what was being said.

Da Silva drew himself up and puffed out his chest, "It is said that Lafitte intends to kidnap you and demand ransom from Dom Pedro if he cannot unearth any treasure here. He is convinced that the royal family will pay handsomely, if only to avoid further scandal." He stared at my stomach in a knowing way. I gave a small moan of distress and the captain attempted to reassure me. "My sword and my men are here in your defence, Dona Lydia." I was not comforted.

"We do not know how many men Lafitte has on that ship — and the guns are trained on the town. I think I am damned."

Dona Serafina wafted on to the veranda at this point, looking thinner and yellower than ever, her rosary beads clanking ominously.

"We must take the path to Ouro Preto at once!" she cried. "It is our only chance. Dona Lydia can be carried in a litter." She sniffed loudly as if to settle the matter. The captain looked doubtful.

"That is impossible," I cried, "I would never survive such a journey." My chaperone did not appear too downcast at such a prospect.

"We must abide by the will of God," she intoned before wafting away. I think I am doomed.

"This is a fine how-de-doo," I moaned. Da Silva looked puzzled but I did not enlighten him. I wished fervently that I could be in a state of well-prepared insensibility. Foreign parts are fruitful of horrors — at least this is true of the more exotic areas. My particular paradise was proving that point. I stared out at the garden where crimson foliage flourished riotously.

I had considered writing a Gothic novel and now I was featuring in a tropical version of one. What awaited me next — a subterranean prison, or a perilous journey over the mountains carried by coarse soldiery?

May 7th

I did not encounter the pirates again for a few days. All I needed to do was send Adelaide into town once more to gather the latest gossip. This she was only too willing to do in the hope of meeting her cavalier again. Da Silva and his men remained *en garde*, polishing their swords assiduously.

Adelaide reported that the townspeople were agog with news and many were terrified. Certain people had already headed for the hills, taking their chances on the *caminho do ouro*. No doubt the count has finally sent for troops but, by the time they arrive, Lafitte and his men will be long gone, taking with them whatever or whomever they choose. It is reported that the pirates are digging on the Beach of the Metal Box — so called because treasure is believed to be buried there. I certainly hope so.

I threw caution to the wind and decided to take a walk to the harbour early on the following morning, accompanied by da Silva, before the heat grew too oppressive. I was feeding the damsel fish and thinking of my Romance when a voice came from behind — a voice with a French accent.

"I like to feed these creatures too. I love the way they nibble your fingers without doing any harm." Lafitte swept me a low bow and instinctively I looked for da Silva. He was standing a few feet away, trying to look unobtrusive.

"Bonjour, Monsieur Lafitte," I said, giving him my best French accent. "I am surprised to see you here. I heard that you were busy at one of Paraty's beaches."

He laughed and dusted his fingers, wiping them delicately on his jacket. "There is a time for everything, madam. My men are working under the supervision of my first officer while I am taking the opportunity to feed the fish. It is indeed opportune that I should meet the most charming lady in Paraty at the same time."

He was certainly trusting for a pirate, if all I had heard about them was true. If only Adelaide had known she would have hot-footed down to the beach. Despite his honeyed words, I did not trust Lafitte. His black eyes remained hooded and cold when he spoke.

"If I can be of any assistance to you, madam, you have only to ask." Another flourish and a bow followed.

I remembered Papa's advice about keeping your enemies close and I gave him a bright smile. "I would be delighted if you called upon us, again, captain. My little household would be honoured."

Lafitte smiled broadly, another smile that did not reach his eyes. "No doubt we will be taking the English tea. I would be charmed." He offered his arm and we made a stately progression around the harbour where da Silva, ignoring my commands as always, was waiting with two of his men. He scowled at Lafitte who relinquished my arm, made another bow and stalked off as if he owned the town — which might soon be the case.

My household was horrified when I told them that Lafitte would pay us another visit, except for Adelaide who was beside herself with anticipation wondering whether Ramirez would accompany his captain. I needed to reduce the strain on my poor self, bearing in mind my condition. My plan was to return to my Romance. After our evening meal, I settled happily with "There Must Be Murder."

CHAPTER
ELEVEN

Apart from issuing the invitation to tea and sending the secret letters to Rio and Ouro Preto, there was nothing to be done about our situation. Doing nothing was always my dear Papa's favourite course whenever anything unpleasant occurred, such as a fall in the Consols or the five percents. Poor Papa's financial speculations were seldom successful, hence his inability to provide for his daughters. It was time to forget the real world and my personal discomforts by returning to my Romance.

"Laurencia was gazing out of her chamber window, suffused with a tender melancholy, when she heard the urgent splashing of oars across the moonlit radiance of the bay."

At this point I heard the angelus bell ringing from the church of Nossa Senhora do Rosario and I recollected Mr Lathom's story of the surly sullen bell sounding at midnight. I decided to incorporate this feature into my own work. The afternoon was taken up with finding a name for the hero and also a suitable title for Laurencia's governess. In a mischievous moment, I decided to call her Serafina. She would be a dark figure in my story, probably a poisoner and a catspaw for the villain — Laurencia's dastardly uncle with the imprisoned wife. The hero's name would be Ferdinand.

I whiled away the time until dinner very successfully in this manner. During our meal the sounds of revelry drifted up from the town's taverns, which were doing tremendous business thanks to Lafitte's crew. Dona Serafina could scarcely eat, she was praying so hard. Adelaide, eyes shining, asked to go into the town again on some pretext but I told her not to be ridiculous. She slunk off looking most put out, while Eufrasia rolled her eyes and da Silva went off to sharpen his sword once more.

I bit down on something hard — a nut, I think, and the carious tooth screamed in protest once again. What a prospect lay before me, dear reader, probable kidnap by pirates, the agonies of childbirth and a visit to the barber surgeon to have a tooth pulled. Worse events had happened to the heroines of Gothic novels, but virtue had always triumphed. If only real life could be like a novel.

I asked myself bitterly what benefit had accrued to me from my attachment to the heir to the throne. My encounters with royalty had always ended in disaster. I was aiming too high, no doubt. I had over-reached my true position in life. I should have taken Mr Darcy's advice and married a curate. Indeed, my spirits were so low at that moment that I would have welcomed the presence of the Prig of Pemberley, and even listened patiently to one of his lectures, if I could have been safely lodged in England.

my back I felt the slight tremor of a sea breeze stealing in from the veranda and fancied that the ghost of Mr Wickham was standing nearby, a sea wraith watching my latest predicament with amusement. I threw a dish across the room and retired to bed.

May 10th

Captain Lafitte and his officers are due to visit us later in the week. In between checking our supplies of tea and instructing Adelaide to bake a batch of rout cakes, which she did most unwillingly (cooking is not one of her duties, but no Portuguese servant or slave understands the recipe), I tried to continue with my Romance.

I allowed myself to dream for a moment that a British man o'war would arrive in the bay to chase off the pesky pirates. Surely Mr Luccombe with his connections could arrange something? I felt very aggrieved that, having been once more recruited to the service of my country, I was now being abandoned. In a more reasonable moment I admitted to myself that nobody could know of my predicament as yet. This led to more recriminations against Dom Pedro who had selected this prison paradise for me.

What would Laurencia do in this situation? Apart from casting a sickly hue over her prospects . . . the writing of "sickly" caused me to have recourse to more herbal tea and lumps of sugared ginger . . . I visualised my heroine in her vaulted chamber with its large

Gothic window. She ventures out to traverse the corridors of her gloomy, crumbling home, idly passing her hand along a panel as the dusk gathers, her fingers press a certain point and a panel silently opens revealing a dark stairwell . . . no doubt this will lead to the cell of the imprisoned wife. At this point, I needed to introduce the evil Serafina who would contrive to lock the heroine in the basement she was unwisely exploring.

Suddenly, Adelaide burst in to the room covered in flour and brandishing a wooden spoon. "The raisins is all maggoty!" she cried. "What am I to do, madam? Everything goes to the bad in this climate." And everyone, I added silently. I went to inspect the kitchen quarters, reluctantly, where I did indeed find weevils or some such thing in among the dried fruit. Fortunately, they appeared to be dead so I instructed Adelaide to add more brandy to the recipe. This may be wasteful but we must be above vulgar economy. Together with the rich egg mixture and a quantity of orange flower water, it would disguise any problems. The pirates at least would be accustomed to fare that was none too fresh. I must remember not to eat anything at the tea party.

The kitchen presented its usual aspect of untidiness with a number of slaves sitting about doing very little, presided over by Eufrasia who proffered the fifth herbal tea of the day. A feeling of powerlessness and weariness washed over me and I began to weep.

I became so agitated that Adelaide and Eufrasia advised me to occupy myself with a calming activity such as netting a purse, otherwise I would harm my health and possibly the baby would be affected. No doubt a highly agitated mother would produce a fractious, mentally impaired child. Oh woe!

My maid produced a design that she had been given by a woman in the town and I settled myself at my desk with the pages of the Romance scattered around me. I commenced knitting a reticule in the shape of a pineapple, the symbol of this town. Unfortunately, the pattern proved to be one of fiendish difficulty, requiring an elaborate three dimensional technique which is quite beyond my limited talents. The top part must be worked in four shades of green, of seven rows each, shading from light to dark. These represent the leaves.

The centre or fruit part is worked in shades of yellow shading to brown, thirty-six rounds of each, ending in green. One part is worked on the right side, another on the left and the green part at the bottom. I had scarcely cast on the stitches a feat requiring three cups of herbal tea to accomplish, when I became hopelessly entangled in the needles, catching my fingers and repeating some of the language learned from the ship's parrot. Far from calming me the attempt rendered me almost apoplectic. Eufrasia took over and finished the article, adding green satin ribbons to the bottom of the pineapple.

While I was still red faced with fury from my herculean efforts, Dona Serafina came stealthily into the room. She moves like a cat. Glancing casually at the papers she spied her own name and snatched up the page. Her English is poor and she was unable to decipher very much but she was clever enough to make out the words "evil" and "Serafina" together.

As I arranged my face and unclenched my jaws she poured out a stream of Portuguese insults, which I understood well enough, having heard Dom Pedro use them frequently. I assume that she believed I was writing to complain about her to the prince. I had not the strength to explain my attempts at fiction.

When she paused for breath I asked her sweetly if she would like to leave my service and return to Rio. Of course, I could not assist her in the present circumstances, but she was free to make her own way. I left her grinding her teeth and yanking her rosary chain as I staggered off and retired to bed with a damp cloth over my face.

CHAPTER
TWELVE

May 12th

The domestic arrangements for Lafitte's visit are now in hand and I am able to return to my Romance for a short while, before considering my own appearance. I reluctantly abandoned an important scene in which Laurencia finally reaches the basement of the castle.

Terrified and in semi-darkness she hears the sound of soft weeping nearby and searches for its source. She is about to discover the unfortunate, imprisoned wife, when a large . . .

"Madam," interrupted Adelaide, "I thought you would like me to prepare a buttermilk wash for you before the visit." She looked pointedly at my hands which I noted with horror were faintly spotted with freckles, and my arms were taking on a similar appearance.

Calling for a mirror, I threw down my pen and hurried to my bedchamber. Elaborate, careful preparations would be needed if my looks were not to frighten the horses — or in this case Lafitte and his men — although in the circumstances that might be no bad thing. There was also the question of dress to consider. There are so few options in this climate.

Eufrasia procured some Grecian-style laced up sandals for my swollen feet. In these, together with a filmy gauze gown (many layered), and an embroidered cloth arranged like a turban on my head, I resembled a fallen nymph after a hasty encounter with Zeus. I must have said this aloud because Adelaide remarked, "Well so you are, madam, in a manner of speaking!" She scampered off and I cursed her for a saucy trollop.

I lay on a couch while the buttermilk paste dried on my skin, plotting the further adventures of Laurencia, and wondering how I should converse with Lafitte. Eufrasia was left to arrange the food and drink while Adelaide preened herself in anticipation. She begged for one of my old gowns, but as she still had the yellow silk from those far off Brighton days, I refused.

"You can scarcely have had much use from the yellow silk," I advised her. "It will be more than adequate for a piratical tea party." My maid immediately began to weep, assuring me that she had worn the gown during our stay in Venice and it had become stained with canal water during her dalliance with the Italian baker. I cannot imagine what she means.

"It's fit only for dusting, madam," she wailed until I relented and gave her a blue and white muslin with tired piping. I will probably never fit into it again.

My maid is determined to impress Ramirez. Perhaps she plans to sail off into the sunset with him leaving me bereft. My problems are endless. In addition, I felt obliged to give another old gown to Eufrasia who was watching from the doorway with a sour expression on her ebony face.

"She can have the yellow silk," Adelaide said. Eufrasia sneered and walked off. The women in this house are most tiresome. At least da Silva does not need to be bribed with my cast off wardrobe, and Dona Serafina wears only black. Adelaide ran off with the gown while I waited patiently for the paste to dry. When she reappeared with the washing water, she was dressed in the blue and white, now with a noticeably lowered bodice. I fear she has lost her senses.

The buttermilk paste has made only a small difference to my skin tone and I devoutly wished for some powder of Pearl of India, which is unobtainable in these parts. Even Eufrasia with her African herbs and potions could not produce such a thing. Not that Africans need whitening potions, of course.

May 14th

On the afternoon of the tea party, I arranged myself on a couch with assistance from the girls under the hostile gaze of Dona Serafina, who proclaimed my sandals to be "indecent" because they revealed bare feet. I advised her that she should be absent from the gathering and she went off to pray at the Chapel of the Generous Woman.

As I expected, the pirate arrived with only five of his officers, prominent among them the first officer Ramirez whose britches were so tight that he could not

94

have digested a wafer let alone a rout cake. Adelaide's eyes almost popped from her head when she beheld this vision. Lafitte and his men bowed low (carefully, in Ramirez' case), as I excused myself for remaining on the couch.

"This is an honour indeed, madam," purred Lafitte, while his men regarded the rout cakes with apprehension. Due to the problem with the weevils, the cakes were somewhat misshapen. Lafitte accepted a cup of English tea with pleasure, while the men toyed with their cups waiting for the alcoholic beverages. Passion fruit liqueur and cachaça fruit punch had been prepared, but I had given strict instructions that they should be served sparingly and that plenty of food should be offered. I did not relish a room full of drunken seafarers.

After the niceties had been observed I decided that I must smoke out Lafitte's real intentions. I began by asking about his early life and childhood, an innocent enough conversation. "I know you are from Saint Domingue, captain. How did you arrive in mainland America?" His eyes took on a soft look for a moment as he harked back to his boyhood on the island with his three brothers. He spoke movingly of his mother.

"She was a French Jewess who came to the Caribbean for a better life. When my father abandoned us we were all very young and my mother raised us in great hardship. I only wish she could have lived to see what I achieved." The statement was made with evident conviction. He was proud of his crimes, but even scoundrels can love their mothers. I recalled Lafitte's desire to retire with a fortune.

"Have you had any success at the beach, monsieur?" This remark caused a strong reaction. Lafitte almost dashed down his china teacup (Royal Doulton English Renaissance) and his face grew dark with fury. "That is no concern of yours, madam, or of anyone in this town," he barked. "As long as we are not molested we will leave you in peace. Otherwise . . ." he looked out of the window in the direction of his heavily armed ship.

Adelaide saw fit to provide a distraction at this point by pressing more cake upon Ramirez. Indeed, she was pressing more than cake upon him until she caught my eye upon her. I knew that da Silva and his men were waiting on the veranda and a guard stood outside the dining room in an extravagantly casual attitude that deceived nobody.

"I am sure the count would like to know of your intentions," I pressed on. Lafitte, his complexion now normal, smiled and pressed a finger against his nose. "You will all know something in due course, madam."

When they departed I retired to the veranda having judged the party a moderate success, although I was none the wiser about Lafitte's intentions. My maid offered to visit the Beach of the Metal Box later.

"I could offer them more rout cakes and listen in to the conversation," she offered but I shooed her away telling her to change into her working clothes.

96

Permanently flushed, she departed to harass the kitchen staff while I returned to my Romance.

Laurencia was in the dungeon area of the castle where she had heard a woman weeping. Pausing at a cell door with a small ~~greeting~~ grating she peered in and saw, by the faint light of a wan taper, the figure of a woman covered in a long black hooded cape. When she called softly through the grating the woman started up in terror.

"Do not be afraid," Laurencia whispered, "I am a friend. What can I do to ~~realize~~ release you?"

The woman approached the grating revealing a worn face with a sweet, sad expression. Her long dark hair was streaked with grey and our heroine could see that her form was thin and malnourished. Laurencia explained that she was the niece and ward of the marquis. The woman looked startled.

"I am Eleanor, the wife of the marquis; he has told the world that I died. I have been locked in here for two years and I wish only to die." The prisoner grasped the bars of the grating and began to sob.

"Why has he done this terrible deed?" gasped Laurencia.

"Because I have not given him a son. He plans to wed a young girl who will give him ~~hair~~ an heir. He cannot bring himself to kill me so he condemns me to a long, lingering death from malnourishment and ill treatment!"

Laurencia's blood froze in her veins as she listened to this terrible tale. She began to realise why the marquis had made her his ward and appeared so fond of her. He planned an unholy alliance with her! This vision filled her with dread and nausea!

"You must leave this place," the woman whispered urgently. "Someone will come soon. His trusted servant brings me scraps of food." She flitted away, wraith-like and resumed her seat, head bowed.

As she groped her way back through the darkness Laurencia vowed to help the unfortunate woman if she could. Was not her own position perilous enough? When she reached the safety of her own chamber, she looked out of the window and saw the marquis riding out to hunt. She was free again for a few hours.

Lunch was eaten in the vast dining hall at an enormous table, where she sat with only Mademoiselle Serafina for company. The woman questioned her closely.

"Where have you been? I have not seen you all morning," suspicion laced her clipped tones. Laurencia answered that she had been reading in a corner of the library. Serafina looked unconvinced and Laurencia escaped back to her room as soon as possible. As soon as Serafina's door closed our heroine slipped quietly out of the castle and made her way to the stables. She had always loved horses. When her father was alive they rode together in the forest near their home every day.

She slipped into the stables inhaling the equine odours and the perfume of hay. The horses were out for the hunt. Only a mare and her foal remained behind. Laurencia buried her face in the mare's warm coat and wept. She wept for her dead parents, her lost home, for the poor woman in her desolate prison and for her own future which appeared bleaker than ever.

"Don't cry!" A voice spoke softly behind her and a hand was placed on her shoulder. She started and turned to see a handsome youth of her own age whom she supposed was the stable boy. He invited her to sit with him on a nearby hay bale. He told her that his name was Ferdinand.

Laurencia poured out her woes, unable to stop. The youth's face was so kind and gentle in its expression and his manner was both respectful yet protective . . .

I found that I was weeping softly over the pages as I wrote, dear reader.

After I had poured out my tale of woe, I was greatly comforted by Ferdinand's compassionate looks. His dark eyes glowed with true feeling as he recounted his own history. I had already ascertained that Ferdinand's refined manners and address indicated that he was no peasant lad assigned to look after the horses.

"I am the son of Count Belladon," he told me. "The marquis killed my elder brother in a duel and my father died soon after, of grief. My mother had died when I was a small child. I am glad that she did not live to see the destruction of our house." He grew silent for a moment, overcome with emotion.

"The marquis appropriated our lands and castle saying that, as a distant relative, he was acting as my guardian. I was sixteen years old and I knew he would kill me if he could. I escaped from the castle with the help of a loyal servant and I lived in the forest for many months — in a charcoal burner's hut. But I knew I would have to return here if I wanted to avenge my family."

I regarded him with amazement. "You have entered the lion's den! Are you not afraid of being recognised?" He laughed bitterly, "I no longer look like a nobleman's son. I am a rough peasant, a stable lad. People see what they expect to see and the marquis does not expect to see his enemy's son in the stables."

After this exchange of sad tales we sat in companionable silence for a while. The realisation that I had finally found a friend and confidante lifted my spirits from the slough of despond into which they had sunk. How would we achieve our aims . . . revenge, escape from the castle for a poor woman — and for me? These questions were insuperable.

My spirits began to sink again and at that moment I heard the shrill tones of Mademoiselle Serafina calling my name. "She is my enemy!" I gasped. "She is in league with the marquis." Ferdinand took my hand and raised it to his lips in a courtly gesture. My heart gave a little leap as I gazed into his beautiful dark eyes. "Try to return here tonight when the castle sleeps. We must devise a scheme to help you and the marquis' wife." I nodded and slipped out of the stables to be confronted by my nemesis.

"What were you doing in there?" she barked, eyeing me in a hostile manner.

"I have been walking for exercise and I slipped in to the stables to pet the mare and her new foal." She brushed me aside and peered into the stables. Seeing no one she seized my arm roughly and hurried me away. I was not to walk in the grounds alone, "for your own safety," she added with an unpleasant smile.

Soon after we returned to the castle I heard the sounds of the marquis and his entourage returning. A message was sent to me requesting my presence at dinner that evening . . . Mademoiselle Serafina came to my door to ensure that I kept this appointment. I had no appetite either for food or the company of my guardian. All my thoughts were of Ferdinand.

As the dishes were uncovered at the table steam rose from the haunch of venison brought back from the hunt. I remembered the imprisoned lady surviving on bread and water and scraps. Her fate was a terrible one. It would have been kinder to kill her outright than to bury her alive. When had she last seen the sun or breathed the summer air? Birds were singing in the garden and late evening sunlight was slanting through the windows of the great hall.

Would I suffer a similar fate if I refused the marquis' demands? Such a thought destroyed my appetite. As I pushed food around on my plate, the marquis frowned and asked if the meal displeased me. He threw off his fur-trimmed, velvet cape and leaned towards me. His eyes were like a cat's or a lion's eyes, pitiless and glinting!

"I hope you are not unwell, Laurencia. You have not eaten." I replied that I had little appetite. Unable to meet his eyes, I mumbled into my uneaten dish of venison, convinced that the marquis would guess that I knew his secrets. I could not keep a tremble from my voice. Absurd! He was the guilty one, yet he revelled in his evil deeds.

He leaned across the table and seized my hand, squeezing it hard. I could scarcely refrain from crying out! "I have a surprise for you, my dear." He signalled to a servant who came forward bearing a gown of rich blue velvet and white silk, lavishly trimmed with silver lace. It was more luxurious than anything in my closet. I saw the Serafina woman's lips tighten in annoyance and envy.

101

"We must improve your wardrobe, as befits your status," the villainous man said. "We have guests tonight at dinner and you will do me honour." He smiled the smile of a predator and released my hand. I stammered my thanks. My guardian did nothing by chance. All his actions were carefully planned to further his ends.

If the gown was meant to display me to advantage to his guests, then my plight was grim indeed. Would he announce his intention to take me as his betrothed? My body turned to ice at the very thought.

At this point I shed a few tears over my heroine's plight — and my own.

I called Adelaide and read the entire piece to her, hoping for a good opinion. She was engrossed by the tale, although I had to explain what a slough of despond might be.

"Is it in Kent?" she asked, "or somewhere near Venice? It's that marshy in those areas." In the circumstances it seemed pointless to ask her if she knew the correct spelling of "insuperable".

When Laurencia returned to her room she found the gown laid out on her bed, together with silver embroidered velvet slippers. With a muffled cry of despair, she flung herself down by the bed and wept piteously. The anguish of her heart was only relieved by a sudden vision of Ferdinand and the tenderness she had glimpsed in his dark eyes.

Gradually she collected herself and began to consider how she might escape from the room to keep her rendezvous with him. But before that longed-for meeting, she must face the ordeal of dinner with the marquis and his guests.

Adelaide interrupted at this point to approve the description of the gown. She thought that Laurencia should have shown more pleasure in receiving it.

"But it has been given to her by an evil man who has designs upon her person," I explained. Adelaide's expression implied that women have to take the rough with the smooth. I have lately realised the truth of that.

CHAPTER
THIRTEEN

The following day, Adelaide persuaded me to take a short walk "for your health, madam." She had returned in one piece from her rendezvous with the first officer and, no doubt, wished to talk about it. Clinging to her arm, I walked with some difficulty over the large, uneven cobblestones laid by slaves almost two hundred years ago. As we walked, I noticed again the curious masonic symbols on the houses and I wondered if the brotherhood really was still powerful in the town.

"They practice foul rites in the catacombs" — that was said unjustly of the early Christians. False rumours are easily spread and I doubted that the Masons indulged in such things; was not Papa one of their number in England? I could not imagine him agreeing to anything untoward, although the Brazilian version might be very different.

I was still pondering on my possible fate, dear reader, and what if anything I might do to save myself. I am sure that when these journals are read by posterity (all the best journals are intended for publication), my readers will appreciate my predicament. Perhaps Adelaide had good news for me, but then I remembered Lafitte's cold eyes and the piratical lust for treasure. Lafitte was no gentleman despite his dandified clothes. I had spied dirt under his fingernails — always a sign of lack of moral fibre and good breeding, according to Papa.

One of the slaves has told Eufrasia that the pirates have returned from the beach having unearthed nothing more than a few rusty muskets. Lafitte is on board his ship no doubt plotting his next move. Will I have to sacrifice my jewels after all? Da Silva said he could not remember where he had buried them, adding hastily that he was speaking in jest. Confound all men! I must rest my swollen feet — soon.

"Do you have anything to tell me?" I asked Adelaide. She eyed me anxiously; "You might offer the captain your jewels in return for a safe passage to Rio, madam."

"My jewels!" I squealed, "my future . . . how can I part with them? You are mad, Adelaide, to suggest such a thing." My maid looked gloomy, saying, "That depends on how much you value your freedom, madam — and mine. We are the only Europeans here, after all." I pointed out that the Portuguese were Europeans too, but she declared that they "don't count because they live here, and it's all their fault." Her logic was somewhat twisted but I could not disagree. Our position is entirely due to Dom Pedro and the court officials.

She caught my arm as I almost tripped and led me back to the house where I was once more installed on the veranda. I gave my maid permission to wander off again to gather information. Eufrasia brought my tea and watched Adelaide depart with a disdainful expression.

"That one no good for work," she opined in her cracked English. I gave her a reproachful look and reminded her that my maid was a personal servant and companion. Eufrasia was not abashed; she is remarkably unsubdued for a slave. She pointed to her nose and said, "slaves hear much — no person see them." She meant of course that no white person pays any attention to a slave. Although her English is not good she hears and sees a great deal. I had no doubt that she was fully aware of our situation. Da Silva wandered in and saluted me in a morose manner.

"It is too quiet, Dona Lydia; it was all very well when those villains were digging up the beach but what are they plotting now? Lafitte will become desperate, and who knows what will happen?" He gave one of his eloquent shrugs that are worth a dozen sentences.

"I have sent Adelaide out again to see what is happening," I told him.

He shrugged again. "What is there to know? They have drunk the taverns dry and paid very little. The townspeople do not venture out after sunset, except for the waterside riffraff."

"And the count . . . what is he doing about this situation?"

Da Silva gave a derisory laugh. "Good taste prevents me from giving a lady my true opinion of the count. Sufficient to say he will do as little as possible. That is the Portuguese way."

I shook my head in disbelief. "They will not allow a pirate from North America to invade their territory, surely? Such a thing is unthinkable."

Da Silva appeared not to have heard me.

"And then there is the problem of the slaves. All this excitement will give them ideas. I trust no one. I have been too long in this country." His words filled me with such alarm that I wished only to retreat into my Romance, but I must remember that I am British. I must do something.

"I shall visit the count," I told him, trying to sound resolute. "I must ascertain his plans for us." Da Silva looked doubtful but went to assemble the guards to escort me. When I told the household of my intentions, reactions varied. Dona Serafina appeared relieved. She would not doubt the word of a Portuguese nobleman. Of course, she is unlikely to be in danger. I cannot imagine the pirates having any use for her.

I felt at a distinct disadvantage being carried over the cobbles in a litter by several perspiring soldiers. The count's wife would not receive me, naturally, but His Excellency admitted me to his library and listened courteously and with obvious disbelief to my story.

"How can I convince you, my lord, that Captain Lafitte intends to carry me off and hold me to ransom?" The count smiled and made a dismissive gesture.

"What would be the point, senhora? He is holding the whole town to ransom but he will not wait for Dom Pedro's money which will arrive with a squadron of soldiers. He will take what he can from us and be gone. The longer he waits, the more dangerous his position becomes."

I could not believe what I was hearing. "The captain can slip anchor and be away within the hour, taking me with him. He has no fear of soldiers. It would be a small matter to seize me and overpower my guards." A small pang of guilt for da Silva attacked me at this point.

"You told me, my lord, that the soldiers you sent for would come from Ouro Preto, not from the sea."

The count mopped his brow. "We cannot hope for salvation by sea. There is not enough time. Never fear, *senhora*. There are enough soldiers here in Paraty to keep you safe." I doubted that. I could not see the count loaning his own guards to protect me. I tried another approach.

"Lafitte has a great advantage, does he not? His guns are trained on the town. He could blow us all to kingdom come." I had great difficulty in translating this last phrase. My Portuguese was cracking under the strain. I wished myself at home with a cup of herbal tea.

The count appeared to understand me but he still disagreed, attributing my "fancies" to my delicate condition. Men can be so irritating. I allowed myself to be conveyed back to the house after enquiring after the health of the countess, the lady who was responsible for the entire female population ostracising me.

As I prepared to leave the count handed me a letter which he said was an invitation from a certain Dom

Luiz dos Carvalhões to stay at the Fazenda Muricama, an estate in the countryside outside the town. Seeing my look of astonishment (I am not familiar with the gentleman), the count assured me that it would be a wise step to take. I thanked him again and left.

When I returned to the house Adelaide had returned. She told me that, "Lafitte won't kidnap you until after the baby is born, madam. It would be too much trouble for him. He wants to wait and see . . ." Her voice trailed away as she realised what she had implied. Everyone will be waiting to see if my baby survives — and the fate of his mother.

The possibility of dying in childbirth is a terrifying one. I recalled mama's vivid descriptions of her tribulations in birthing five daughters. How could I have been so unfortunate? I became so overwrought that Eufrasia produced a charm used by her people as protection in childbirth. Tears poured down my cheeks as I accepted it. I did not wish to know what was in the tiny bundle attached to a string, but would it be effective for an Englishwoman? I am not an African tribeswoman. When I recollected myself, I returned to my Romance . . .

It took all her courage to advance along that black void, but after a few minutes of walking she felt the ground rise as if going uphill. The tunnel widened out into a large chamber lit by flares in large sconces on the walls. Her amazement at this sight quickly turned to fear as she realised that a human agent must be at work nearby.

To her horror she heard footsteps approaching. As she stood rigid with fear holding the candle aloft, she was astonished and overjoyed to see Ferdinand enter the chamber from another tunnel entrance. He greeted her joyfully, but Laurencia was so overcome after her ordeal that she sank to the ground in a swoon, allowing her candle to roll away. Ferdinand hastened to raise her up and she found that she was clinging to him and weeping softly. He released her gently and explained how he came to be in the tunnel.

"There is a ruined chapel not two miles from here. I found the entrance to the tunnel there and followed it knowing it would lead to the castle."

"I entered from my own chamber," Laurencia replied. "I found the hidden door, but I am afraid that my absence will be discovered if that woman Serafina comes to check on me." Ferdinand reassured her that it was unlikely to happen. "She will not imagine that you can escape from a locked chamber, so why will she check? Come; we must find some other windings from this tunnel. Perhaps one of them will lead to the imprisoned lady."

"But how will we release her if we find her?" Ferdinand showed her the carpet bag he carried, which contained various instruments and tools. Laurencia was full of admiration for his foresight and determination.

They set off carefully along the tunnel while Ferdinand felt along the walls until he found a small opening leading to a smaller tunnel. He took Laurencia's hand and led her along the tunnel.

I paused at this point for more herbal tea. When I read this piece to Adelaide she pronounced it sufficiently creepy and "guaranteed to shiver anyone's timbers." She has begun to use nautical expressions since developing a passion for a pirate.

CHAPTER
FOURTEEN

July 1st

It is barely ten o'clock in the morning and already my muslins are glued to my back. I called Eufrasia to fan me. She watches me with that inscrutable look, those unfathomable black eyes I know so well. The slaves — how they must hate us . . . and the Indians too. The whites have taken their land and slaughtered them in their thousands. Da Silva watches them with a brooding expression.

"See, Dona Lydia, they are plotting rebellion in the shade of the mango trees. He patted his sword. "Only this stands between you and annihilation." Da Silva gets pleasure from this kind of remark. He is altogether too full of himself.

"If the Portuguese had not stolen their land and enslaved them we would have nothing to fear," I replied.

"And the English, would they have acted differently?" he sneered. "What are they doing in India and Africa? I fell silent having no answer to that. The baby kicked me as if to warn me to keep quiet. My time is close and I am fearful. If only my practical sister Lizzie was here — or even Mama with her vapours. I am so very far from home. Only Adelaide, loyal Adelaide is here with her reassuring cockney phrases. Following Dona Serafina's suggestion she is bringing me coffee sweetened with molasses. The smell of it almost causes me to heave my stomach. I would give anything for a cup of Twining's souchong with milk. I have taken too much herbal tea.

I confess that I have moments of despair especially when I wake in the night, in the whispering, tropical night and the ghosts of my past misdemeanours cluster around the bed, twitching and muttering reproachfully. Then I wake with a start or a scream.

Sometimes, I see Wickham in his scarlet regimentals sitting on the end of the bed rolling dice. He looks unnaturally pale, as one would expect. He is deceased, after all. He waves a pack of cards in my direction in a manner half amused, half threatening. Adelaide says these are the fancies of pregnancy; Eufrasia says they are omens from the *orishas*. These are her strange African gods. She goes down to the beach at night and makes offerings to Iemanjá, the goddess mother of the waters.

Meanwhile, everyone here complains and cries and yells day and night. Eufrasia, strange, unsettling Eufrasia, puts her fingers in her ears to block out what she calls the white laughter of the mulattos.

"How can laughter be white?" I asked her. "You are being fanciful, my girl." She shakes her head and declares that their laughter is not like the laughter of black people. The blacks hate the mulattos who control much of the trade here in Paraty. Many of the sugar barons in the Paraiba valley have mixed race wives and children.

I have a fancy to accept the invitation and travel up to the estate of Dom Luiz dos Carvalhões at Fazenda Muricama. I could be carried in a litter. There is no one from the court to prevent me. I am under the protection of the Count of Paraty but he has urged me to leave the town. I would like my child to be born on the Fazenda. Adelaide complained loudly when I told her of my intentions. She hates travelling in this heat and, of course, she will be separated from the first officer.

August 20th

It is settled: When the time comes I will travel by litter to the Fazenda. Adelaide and Eufrasia will attend me. Dona Serafina, my dragon lady chaperone will accompany us with a midwife and da Silva's body guards.

October 4th

When my time drew near and after a good deal of the usual fussing and feuding among the slaves and the bodyguards, we departed a day late after twenty-four hours of a heavy downpour — the type of weather da Silva described as "*está chovendo barba de sapo.*" He obligingly translated this as "it's raining frogs' beards." I took a supply of custard tarts for which I have lately

114

developed a craving. I fear it will be some time before I can resume my Romance.

Dom Luiz greeted me with great courtesy when we arrived at the Fazenda Muricama. He is an older gentleman, a widower whose sister acts as hostess for him. Dona Caterina was also gracious and welcoming. Whatever her opinion of my condition, she and her brother were devoted to the royal family and their service. They had been commanded to offer me hospitality and they fulfilled this task implicitly.

After I had rested, I was shown around the estate which is a delightful oasis in the Atlantic rain forest. It is a self-contained world growing its own food.

"We bring only wine from the outside world," Dom Luiz smiled, "and books whenever I can obtain them." In addition to the main house there is a chapel, workshops, stables and huts for the fifty slaves who work the estate. The fertile land yields every kind of tropical fruit.

Although they are far from civilisation — even Paraty seems a hotbed of culture in comparison — they are content with their lot. Dom Luiz admitted that it has been many years since he saw the shores of his native Portugal. As for me, I am content to be away from the town and the sea and hovering pirate crew for a while.

October 11th

For a few days everything was calm and pleasant, then I experienced spasms of pain and knew that my time was almost come. On one occasion I was seized with pain as I passed the chapel. I leaned against the chapel wall for support just as my host's chaplain opened the door. He took in my situation, gasped with horror, bolted inside and slammed the door. Eufrasia appeared at that moment, spat cheerfully at the door and assisted me back to the house. The pains subsided for a while and I sat on the veranda as the sky darkened with storm clouds and the air became so heavy it felt as if it was bearing down on my shoulders.

As night fell, bonfires were lit around the Fazenda, surrounded by the fifty slaves singing and chanting in their African language. Distant rolls of thunder were rumbling over the hills. Perhaps the slaves were invoking Xangô, the god of thunder. Between the singing and the chanting and the noise from the sky, my labour pains seized me in an agonizing, iron grip.

"I am so afraid!" I cried to Dona Serafina, who for once looked almost compassionate.

"Pray, pray my child!" she commanded. "Pray for a safe delivery." And I prayed, between the singing and the chanting and the crashing in the heavens, I prayed and cursed and howled. The midwife made me lie on my side with my legs drawn up for as long as possible, "To preserve your modesty."

Dona Serafina set up a portable shrine to the Virgin and was clicking her rosary beads loudly. I could hear Adelaide arguing on the veranda because she had been refused admission to my room. I could hear my own voice shrieking, but it was as if everything was coming from a great distance.

116

When the baby was finally delivered and had been washed and swaddled, Dona Serafina snatched him away and covered him with an array of holy medals, Solomon's seals and other lucky charms before hurrying with him to the little chapel where the monk will baptise him in the Romish faith . . . "To save his soul," she mutters with a furtive look in my direction. Of course she means because he is a bastard and his mother is a Protestant heretic, but I am too exhausted to care.

At least he is a *royal* bastard and kings look after their own. He will be named Sebastian after the patron saint of Rio — Sebastião in the Portuguese tongue. Dom Pedro chose this and I agreed, asking only for the name of Bennet to be included in the list of saints' names. A black slave wet nurse has been found for him. Adelaide thinks this is disgusting but it is the custom here.

CHAPTER
FIFTEEN

October 25th

I do not know how the news of my son's birth and our survival in good health leaked out from the Fazenda. We feel so far from everywhere, yet still people creep in and out of places, forests notwithstanding.

As I began to regain my strength and my body returned to an approximation of its former self (I have foresworn the custard tarts), worrisome rumours began to reach us. Parties of armed men have been sighted in the forest on occasions. Da Silva and his men went out on patrol but found nothing. Nevertheless, I am uneasy. I know we have to return to Paraty soon; we cannot impose on the hospitality of Dom Luiz indefinitely. Captain da Silva assures me that there will be no problem. The journey is not so long ("as the crow flies, madam," said Adelaide). Little Sebastian is flourishing; there is no reason to delay.

Of course, most of the rumours come from the slaves on the Fazenda relayed to me by Eufrasia. The slaves go about the forest gathering all manner of flora and fauna. Da Silva is dismissive of "slave chatter," declaring them to be full of fancies and superstitions.

"Surely," I protested, "it is not a matter of superstition. Either they saw and heard something or they did not?" He shrugged and returned to cleaning his musket. "We saw nothing on our patrol." In short, we are preparing to leave in a few days and while Adelaide and Eufrasia prepare for the journey I can return to my Romance which has been neglected of late. In these uncertain times it is good to have another string to one's bow. According to Dom Luiz there are stirrings of revolution in various parts of the country. Many people wish to gain independence from Portugal. Naturally, I have heard no news from England for many weeks. One can only hope that Napoleon has not returned from exile once again.

As the two young people crept along the tunnels towards the dungeon where the imprisoned lady was held, Laurencia felt that the chill, heavy air was diffused with a solemnity and terror that vibrated in thrilling sensations upon her heart. The apprehension of new terrors and misfortunes kept them silent as they progressed, while Laurencia clung firmly to Ferdinand's hand.

Even that stout-hearted youth was affected by the sense of melancholy dread that filled these lower regions. He stopped for a moment, fancying that he heard a noise. Could it be pursuers — or something unnatural?

"Were I inclined to superstition," he murmured to his companion, "I might imagine all kinds of nightmarish things." Laurencia gasped and he squeezed her hand reassuringly. At that moment there was a loud rushing sound and numerous birds, bats and rooks, swept through the tunnel. The two flung themselves down and used their arms to shield themselves. Laurencia could not prevent a muffled scream escaping her lips. Ferdinand shooed the birds away, thankful that there was no human agent at work. He raised Laurencia up and gently urged her on.

When they reached the lady's prison she was at first astonished and fearful to see them. Even after her cell door was unlocked she had to be coaxed outside. Enveloped in a dark cloak and hood, she was helped along the tunnel leading to the open air but their progress was painfully slow. The young couple supported the lady as best they could but her condition was so weak that Ferdinand grew more and more anxious. The first rays of dawn were appearing as they reached the waiting horses and galloped away towards the forest. Laurencia felt a kind of exultation knowing that she had escaped from the castle and her guardian's malign household. If only they could avoid recapture.

As they fled towards the remote abbey where they hoped to find sanctuary, the night mists rolled away and the green curtain of the forest was penetrated by slivers of ethereal silver light. Within the hour the first ruddy gleams of sunlight appeared. They were exposed to the view of anyone about in the forest. Ferdinand was concerned that bandits might inhabit the interior and behind them lurked the fear of pursuit by the marquis and his men. Surely they would have been missed by now?

Soon they spied the lonely, turreted edifice perched on the side of a mountain in the distance — the abbey where they hoped to find succour. "We must make haste!" cried Ferdinand, urging on the horses. The lady swayed in the saddle, exhausted and would have fallen if she had not been tied securely. When they reached the abbey Ferdinand pulled vigorously on the bell rope and they were soon admitted to the courtyard.

There is a pause here for tea.

Adelaide expressed no interest in hearing my latest chapter. She prefers to admire baby Sebastian.

November 10th

When we finally bade farewell to Dom Luiz and his household and set out for Paraty, I felt in my bones that I was facing great changes in my life. Now that I was a mother I doubted that I would be of interest to Dom Pedro. Indeed, I have heard that he is consoling himself with a new young mistress.

How soon would I be able to leave Brazil and where would I go? I told Adelaide that I had a fancy to settle somewhere warm but not too hot on the continent, conveniently away from England. "Not Venice!" we cried in unison. Perhaps Italy would be good, especially Florence — although I have heard that it is an unhealthy spot.

In the meantime there was the problem of Captain Lafitte to be faced. I imagined the pirate crew confined to their cramped quarters on board ship enduring galleon fever, and anxious to get their grappling hooks away while their captain's black eyes flashed alarmingly. An icy chill ran up my spine despite the heat.

I opened the curtains and poked my head out of the litter and called to da Silva, "Captain! Turn right . . . we must go to Ouro Preto." The little procession folded in on itself in an untidy heap. The litter tipped slightly sideways and baby Sebastian began to wail. Da Silva hurried up gesticulating wildly.

"What is this, Dona Lydia? You cannot want to travel up a rocky track fit only for mules. We must return to the coast. Ouro Preto is far too distant."

"No," I said; "I have a feeling of impending doom — a premonition if you will. This journey will not end well."

He gestured at the soldiers and slaves standing around. "This is a large enough party to face down any opposition. We will not meet an army in this forest." Defeated, I disappeared behind the curtains and we resumed our journey. I put my head in my hands feeling as dismal as baby Sebastian who continued to grizzle in the background.

"Don't take on madam," urged Adelaide. Her spirits are high, I suspect she anticipates meeting the first officer Ramirez once again. Sebastian's wet nurse — a pert quadroon in a frilly skirt — sniggered at my downcast looks until Adelaide glared at her. The girl is more afraid of the maid than of her mistress.

November 15th

Despite my apprehension we did in fact reach Paraty unscathed; finding the house only lightly covered with dust and my voguish French mirror showing signs of rust due to the climate. That evening, despite my weariness, I ardently wished to return to my Romance.

When the house was quiet I sat at my desk and took up my quill.

Ferdinand and Laurencia were relieved to be within the walls of the monastery. Their charge was safely in the care of the dispensary, but they knew that their respite was temporary. It would surely not be long before the marquis and his men would reach their place of safety.

"We must leave here as soon as possible," Ferdinand told his companion. She became pale and her eyes filled with tears. "How can we hope to outrun our pursuers, hampered as we are with a sick woman?" he continued.

Laurencia made no reply, merely looked at him imploringly. "Perhaps we could leave her here; she would be in safe hands. The marquis will surely not violate the sanctuary of the monastery. I believe we are his intended quarry."

"The marquis is capable of anything," declared Ferdinand. "Surely you and I know the truth of that?" A tear ran down her cheek unheeded. Ferdinand smiled sadly at her, noting the sweetness and fine expression of her voice and her distinguished and graceful figure. He took her hand and kissed it gently, her voice still vibrating in his heart.

"You are like a Grecian nymph! he exclaimed. "Laurencia, before we flee again we should be married — here in the monastery chapel. I wish to devote my life to you whether it be long or short." Laurencia found herself unable to speak; she was overcome with emotion and joy.

The two young people embraced and Ferdinand kissed her tenderly. "Let us ask the Abbot to perform the ceremony tomorrow morning."

"Whatever happens now," sighed Laurencia, "I will have had this unspeakable joy."

Their nuptials were celebrated soon after dawn on the following day. Attended by an austere congregation of monks they knelt before the altar, the bride clad in a simple white gown and veil provided by the Abbott. The marquesa was considered too sick to attend the ceremony.

The soft, golden candle flames illumined the bleakness of early morning in the gloomy chapel. Wan daylight filtered through the stained glass windows as the monks intoned the words of the mass. Ferdinand placed his mother's ring on Laurencia's finger, which he had concealed on a string about his neck. The sound of horses' hooves could be heard faintly through the walls.

The brethren had barred the heavy wooden doors of the chapel and a great hammering ensued with shouts and curses. The Abbot calmly continued with the service while Laurencia almost collapsed with terror. As soon as the ceremony was concluded the pair turned to face the congregation as man and wife, just as three men burst through an unguarded side door, the marquis at their head. With a loud curse he raised his pistol, but Ferdinand had pulled his bride behind the heavy wooden bulk of a confessional. Ever alert to danger he pulled a pistol from inside his jerkin and returned shots. The shouts and cries of the monks as they rushed about impeded the men accompanying the marquis, while some monks managed to secure the door. As the confusion continued Ferdinand raised his head from the hiding place and shot the marquis in the arm. He immediately returned the shot and Laurencia fell to the ground. She had involuntarily followed Ferdinand from his hiding place.

Ferdinand, believing his beloved to be dead, loosed a volley of shots at the marquis before leaping across the intervening pews in pursuit. The marquis limped away as fast as he could, having been shot in the leg. As the two met up outside the chapel the bare hillside rang with two final shots that left the marquis dead on the ground and Ferdinand badly wounded.

"Laurencia, my beloved!" were his last words as consciousness left him. The first rays of sunlight were glinting on the purple hills beyond the forest and birds began to sing in the green covert.

As I paused to rest my aching hand I heard a noise.

"Who is there?" I called, expecting Eufrasia to come gliding in from the veranda . . . No one entered but I heard a slight movement outside. "Oh do come in, girl!" I called, but Eufrasia still did not appear. Instead, the lace curtain parted and there stood Adelaide's beau in all his glory. I looked him up and down and remarked, "Do you always appear in a lady's boudoir heavily armed, sirrah?"

Not a whit abashed Ramirez clanked his heels together and wished me good day.

"I would be obliged, madam, if you would accompany me to the ship, at the captain's request. There is a litter waiting outside. Your servants and the baby are already accommodated."

"What!" I cried. "How dare you, sir? Are you inviting me to be kidnapped? What if I refuse?"

"Then I will be obliged to throw you over my shoulder," he replied in a nonchalant manner, carefully moving his weapons to one side. This gave me pause.

What was happening; why had Adelaide and the others not put up some resistance? I had not heard as much as a shriek. Of course, Adelaide was totally unable to resist Ramirez and would have followed him anywhere. A baby's cry reached me at that moment. Baby Sebastian was being taken away! I rushed outside closely followed by Ramirez.

Two pirates awaited me and they quickly took my arms and almost threw me into the litter where I landed in Adelaide's lap. "Where is the baby?" I demanded. She indicated another litter waiting alongside. "He is in there with the nursemaid."

"But where is da Silva — and the bodyguard?"

My maid shrugged. "They have been rendered helpless. Tom . . . Mr Ramirez put something in their midday *cachaça*." She attempted to look shamefaced but failed. I regarded her, shocked to the core.

"I cannot believe that you would assist those wretches, Adelaide. What will become of us — of the baby? You have taken leave of your senses." My maid rushed to her lover's defence.

"They mean you no harm, madam. As soon as a ransom is paid they will release you." I noticed that she had not included herself in these arrangements,

"What will you do, my girl? Surely you do not intend to go off with that pirate? It will end very badly for you . . . and after all I have done for you." I gave a snort of outrage. Adelaide remained silent while another thought struck me. "Where is Dona Serafina?"

"She hid from the pirates. They did not look for her."

"And Eufrasia?"

126

Adelaide shrugged again. "They were not bothered with the slaves." If Dona Serafina escaped surely she would alert the count. A rescue expedition would be mounted. Somehow I could not convince myself of this. Captain da Silva and his men will rescue us eventually, I told myself but, again, I remained unconvinced. We were being jolted along none too gently by the pirates.

CHAPTER
SIXTEEN

December 5th

We were bumped and hurried on our way to the harbour where we were bundled onto Lafitte's ship. The glimpses I had through the curtains of the litter revealed a complete absence of soldiers — either the count's men or my own bodyguard. Doubtless they were still sleeping off the *cachaça*. As I descended from the litter Lafitte swept me a low bow. I was not greatly diverted. His men glowered at us as we passed them.

The pirate leader made a great deal of the fact that he had made his own cabin available to me, the baby and the maids. I ignored this.

"How dare you seize us in this manner?!" I screeched at him. "You will hang for this, and your crew with you." I heard my voice shake a little. I was close to tears of fury and terror — and Lafitte knew it. He gave me one of his crooked smiles that did not reach his cold eyes.

"Stay calm, madame, all will be well. Let us discuss matters in my cabin. May I offer you some refreshments?" I knew very well that the only discussion would be about money and how much my person would be worth. Baby Sebastian began to wail loudly at this point as if to emphasise the point.

When we were settled in the cabin, Lafitte leaned towards me in an unpleasantly confiding manner. "I must tell you, madame, that I am on a special quest. I am in search of the Fountain of Youth!" I laughed, assuming he was making a jest.

"We would all like to find that, sir."

Lafitte shifted impatiently in his chair. "It is said that the Fountain of Youth is hidden somewhere in these parts."

I sneered politely. "Yes, it could be the pineapples or pomegranate juice or the *cachaça*, or the açaí berries or a mixture of all three." He glared at me and took a slurp of brandy from a silver hip flask.

"I have a document that will lead me to the place where it is to be found. You are young, Madame Lydia, and you do not understand. When your beauty begins to fade and wrinkles furrow your brow you will not laugh at the idea of a fountain of youth. You will seek it in vain in a tub of cream."

This speech was delivered in Lafitte's charming French accent — his only asset — but it puzzled me. "It is kind of you to describe me as beautiful, captain, but I had not thought you to be so vain." He looked even more annoyed and I felt Adelaide's shoe attempting to kick me discreetly.

"It is not simply a question of vanity!" he roared, leaping up from his chair and clutching the table for support. "I need time . . . more time to recoup my losses. I need to roll back the years." He began muttering to himself and searching feverishly among the papers heaped on the table before turning to me again.

"I need a fail-safe plan, a second string is the English expression, I believe. The Portuguese will pay handsomely for you and your child but . . . but if I cannot buy back youth I shall at least be wealthy." I remained silent and after a few more slurps of brandy Lafitte left us and went above deck. I concluded that he wished for both money and youth and was not sure of receiving either — hence his bad mood. The nursemaid began to sob with fright and even Adelaide began to look uncomfortable. I silently cursed Lafitte for a ruthless, cross-grained villain.

"I am not convinced that the Portuguese will pay a ransom, or possibly not enough to satisfy Lafitte. We must contrive to escape somehow." Adelaide received this announcement with horror. Perhaps her faith in the handsome first officer was beginning to waver.

"How can we do that, madam? It will be impossible — and with the baby too." A difficult half hour ensued as I attempted to calm everyone. Eventually, Adelaide begged to be allowed to go up on deck "to look around."

"That would be most unwise," I told her. "You will be at the mercy of pirate ruffians." She blushed and looked coy and I realised she expected to meet the first officer. I waved my hand. "Oh, go, Adelaide. Perhaps you will learn something to our advantage, but I doubt it." She departed quickly and Sebastian began to wail. My spirits sank into my boots, but I must not indulge in a fit of the vapours.

When my maid eventually returned her cheeks were crimson and her hair stood almost on end, giving her the appearance of one of the Bacchae after an initiation ceremony. She claimed to have news from Tom. "Well, out with it girl!" I cried. Adelaide tried to compose herself.

"Tom did say that he might be able to assist us in return for something of great value."

"Such as?"

"Well, I mentioned your necklace from the Prince Regent and he became quite excited." I had no doubt of that. So I was to hand over my most valuable asset to a handsome ruffian who might or might not effect our release. "And what do you gain from all of this?" I asked my maid.

She blushed again. "Tom has offered to take me with him when the ship sails for North America."

"With my necklace as your booty? I cannot believe such betrayal." It was Adelaide's turn to look outraged.

"I did it for you and the baby, madam. I don't trust that Lafitte and I don't trust Dom Pedro neither." She repeated her favourite saying, that I was not lucky where gentlemen were concerned. This was certainly true but Lafitte was not a gentleman, and neither was Dom Pedro for all his blue blood.

"Lafitte will scarcely allow us to escape from under his nose."

Adelaide leaned forward and whispered in my ear. "Tom says that the men are tired of Lafitte and his strange ways. They think he is cracked in the head and they want to return to the United States. Tom will take over the ship and lock Lafitte in the hold. They will probably put him ashore on an island somewhere." I gave her a speculative look.

"They will probably do the same to you, my girl. Women are considered unlucky on board ships and pirates are very superstitious, I have heard. There is an island off the coast of Mexico called Isla Mujeres where pirates are wont to leave their women for long periods. Is that what you desire?"

She shrugged this aside and we turned to the problem of retrieving the necklace which was buried in the garden of the villa. We decided to send a message to Dona Serafina somehow. She could bring the necklace to the ship. The pirates were unlikely to molest her. Adelaide went off to arrange this with Tom.

I would have enjoyed being a fly on any nearby wall when Dona Serafina met Tom Ramirez and handed over the necklace. Serafina was fluent in Spanish and would no doubt have had much to say.

December 4th

Only a day later, after the sounds of much scuffling and swearing were heard above our heads, we were told that Tom had taken over the ship and the captain was locked in the hold. My necklace lay winking in the lamplight on Lafitte's table as Tom Ramirez admired it.

"I trust you are satisfied, sir, and that you will release us as soon as possible?" He nodded, then said that he would put us ashore at a suitable place. We were already heading out of the bay and Paraty was rapidly receding from view. Alarming visions of the Isla Mujeres swam before my eyes. This villain would betray us like the others of his kind. At that moment Dona Serafina burst into the cabin escorted by two members of the crew who appeared to be mortally afraid of her. Perhaps she had put a curse on them.

"Release these ladies at once!" she barked at Hernandez. "A vessel from Rio is entering the bay in pursuit. It is fully armed and it will be the end of you if you are caught. You will hang from the yardarm of your ship." Ramirez' charm slipped visibly at this and he began to curse volubly. "I am an American citizen!" he exclaimed. Dona Serafina replied that he was a pirate and a criminal in Portuguese waters and he would hang regardless. When Adelaide attempted to take his hand he threw her across the cabin.

In the ensuing fracas we all clambered on to the deck aided by the crew who could not wait to be rid of us. Sure enough, a ship was sighted on the horizon, but we could not tell whether it was friend or foe.

We were rowed to shore while the pirate ship prepared to leave once more. On shore Dona Serafina hastened us away from the direction of our house to the lonely Chapel of the Generous Woman on the edge of town. When I protested she said we would be safe there.

"What have we to fear now?" I asked. "The pirates have gone and a Portuguese ship approaches. We are saved." Dona Serafina looked unimpressed.

"Ask *her* for the reason." She pointed accusingly at Adelaide who sheepishly produced my necklace from her pocket. She had managed to seize it from its pouch while Ramirez was otherwise occupied.

"When Ramirez realises his loss he will come back. He is protected by the count who, I am afraid, has been in collusion with the pirates for his own financial ends." Dona Serafina's pain at this evidence of Portuguese perfidy was palpable. Adelaide protested that she had taken the necklace for my benefit and because Ramirez had thrown her aside.

At this point I confessed that the necklace was worthless paste which I had caused to be made in Rio. The real necklace was in the care of the Luccombes. Overcome by these events, I collapsed in an empty confessional while Dona Serafina and the nurse resorted to keeping baby Sebastian quiet by mixing a few drops of brandy in his milk. Serafina is proving remarkably useful after all.

Suffice to say, dear reader, that after an anxious few hours, a ship commissioned by Mr Luccombe docked at Paraty to rescue us. At the sight of this vessel I felt relief and joy that was inexpressible. We had been within inches of a very unpleasant fate ... Dona Serafina said that we should give thanks to the Generous Woman whose chapel had been our refuge, and for once I agreed with her.

I was delighted to find Mr Luccombe himself on board the ship. He scooped us up and we were soon bound for Rio de Janeiro, stopping only to collect our belongings, and Eufrasia. I regretted not bidding farewell to da Silva but there was no sign of my bodyguard.

"Still drunk, I expect," commented Adelaide.

"I could not let a servant of the British Crown fall into the hands of a Yankee pirate!" Mr Luccombe twinkled at me, while simultaneously admiring baby Sebastian. As we were sailing away from our troublesome paradise I quizzed Adelaide about her plans with Ramirez.

"Were you really going to live on board ship with the first mate, after all I have done for you, Adelaide?" I had, after all, paid her wages quite regularly and enabled her to see the world, if unwillingly. She had the grace to look shamefaced.

"I was that smitten with him, madam, I would have followed him anywhere until I heard what the pirates planned to do. I couldn't let anything happen to you and the baby." I patted her arm.

"You did well, Adelaide, and I am not ungrateful." I resolved to pass one or two of my gowns on to her when the time was right.

"Will we be going home now, madam?" she asked in a hopeful tone.

"I anticipate a return to England, in the first instance," I told her. "My contract is finished and I am not wanted at the Portuguese court unless Dom Pedro has a change of heart."

My maid regarded the baby who was sleeping peacefully. "It all depends on the little one, doesn't it?" We shall see.

CHAPTER
SEVENTEEN

December 6th

After a long absence, or so it seemed to me, I returned to my Romance. I had left Ferdinand and Laurencia in dire straits. They were both at death's door but I could scarcely leave them there. My readers would expect a satisfactory conclusion, the triumph of good over evil. I took up my pen again, relieved to have some quiet time at last.

When Ferdinand awoke he saw that he was within the plain white walls of the monastery's infirmary. Rows of bottles and containers ringed the room. Despite the pain that racked his body, he recognised the marquesa, Lady Eleanor hovering by his bed, her face furrowed with sorrow and strain. Realisation dawned upon him and he tried to sit up while uttering an agonised cry,

"Laurencia, Laurencia my love!" The lady, now risen from her own sickbed put out her hand to soothe his brow. Ferdinand sank back in pain and despair and one of the brothers hurried up to his bed, urging him to remain still or his wound would open and bleed again.

"Do not fret, dear boy," the lady assured him, "Laurencia is alive. She lies yonder." She pointed to a bed on the far side of the room. Ferdinand turned his head and saw his beloved lying, still and pale, with her arm heavily bandaged. The infirmarian told him she was merely sleeping. "She will recover, as will you, with rest and care."

The three unfortunates spent many weeks recovering at the monastery until they regained their strength. Their joy grew day by day as they realised that their enemy was no more and the prospect of a long and happy life lay before them.

In due course they received an edict from the ruler of those lands that restored Ferdinand's estates and title. Many of the men who had been in service with the marquis came to offer fealty to their lawful ruler, and they received a pardon. When the little procession eventually set out for the castle, the joy felt by the two lovers was unspeakable. Now man and wife, they walked hand in hand into their domain to receive the cheers and greetings of their retainers. The Lady Eleanor accompanied them and became an honoured member of the household, living out the rest of her days in peace. However, the privations and sufferings of her imprisonment had fatally undermined her constitution and she did not live long.

They had found Mademoiselle Serafina locked in her room. She had barricaded the door with heavy furniture but Ferdinand ordered his men to force an entry. As they burst into the room the evil woman screamed curses at them as she retreated towards the open casement. Before they could restrain her she threw herself out of the window into the moat below. Her broken body was seen sinking under the water.

Laurencia looked on in horror. "Despite her cruelty to me I would not have wanted her die in such a manner." She shuddered and hid her face in Ferdinand's shoulder.

He held her close and said, "No doubt she preferred such a death to the years she would have spent in the dungeons of this castle. Do not mourn her, my love!"

Ferdinand and Laurencia took up their responsibilities and ruled their lands wisely for many years and were beloved by their subjects. Their descendants rule those lands to this day.

When I laid down my pen I could not help shedding more tears for Laurencia and Ferdinand who had become as familiar to me as members of my family. Their trials and tribulations compared with my own but the outcome for me was less certain. However, self-pity must be avoided, it is so unbecoming. There will be a satisfactory outcome, eventually, I am certain of this. Have I not escaped from pirates, Freemasons, troublesome princes and all manner of ridiculous situations?

After I read the final part of the story to Adelaide she claimed that my "horrid" tale had given her nightmares.

"As if we had not suffered enough in reality," she moaned. I forbore to mention the part she had played in our problems. After all, she had finally come to her senses regarding the wretched pirate Tomas.

December 28th

Dom Pedro greeted me with affection when we met on Christmas Day at the house in the hills above Rio which I had briefly inhabited before Paraty. He admired little Sebastian, pronouncing him to be a fine boy, before returning him to the wet nurse who took him back to the nursery. He brought gifts for his son, a charming coral and ivory rattle and a small, solid gold drinking cup engraved with the royal crest and the letter S. He did not remain long with us and his parting remark was one of embarrassed apology, "for all the trouble you have endured because of our relationship." He departed, assuring me of his utmost and enduring regard for my person. It was a strange speech, I thought. After all, I had entered into the arrangement willingly enough. It was obvious that Dom Pedro was trying to convey a message to me, but, being royal, he would prefer one of his minions to do the deed.

The minion was not long in coming. A few days later Dom Joaquim de Vilhena, a court official, came to call. He began with the greatest formality.

"I am delighted to inform you that it has pleased his majesty to confer on your son the title of Baron Monserrat. He will receive the education and upbringing of a noble, eventually taking his place as a court official." Dom Joaquim bowed and I returned the bow. Then he explained that *my* presence would not be required.

"His Royal Highness is sure that you would not wish to incommode the royal family. In view of your short contract with Dona Leopoldina it would be appropriate if you now made plans to leave Brazil. Your son will remain behind." He bowed again and sat down mopping his forehead with a large lace-edged handkerchief.

I sat as if turned to stone as this news was given to me. It was not totally unexpected, and I did indeed want to return to England, but I had thought to take my child with me — or had I? How would I explain him at Longbourn or Pemberley? What could I offer him in comparison to the grandeur of the court? A sudden pang of sadness pierced my heart. Sebastian was my son and I would not see him grow. We would never become close to each other. It was not fair!

Meanwhile, Dom Joaquim was telling me that all my expenses would be met. He stood up and handed me a long mahogany box embossed with Dom Pedro's crest, suggesting that I should leave "soon." Dona Serafina would arrive to take the baby to the palace with his wet nurse. Everything had been prepared. He made another elaborate bow and departed.

The box remained on my lap for several minutes after his departure until Adelaide gently removed it and opened the lid. A magnificent diamond collar sparkled up at us. I had been paid off. My maid patted my hand, "Upon my word, madam, this will keep you in comfort for many a year." Eufrasia peered at the stones and said nothing.

Later, as I sat at the window watching the violent rose and gold afternoon light dying into indigo, Eufrasia came to me. "There might be a way to get him back. I can help you, lady."

I am to accompany my slave to a *candomblé* gathering. "What will happen?" I asked her. I was apprehensive, but Eufrasia smiled. "We give a party and the gods come!"

For the first time since she entered my employ, Adelaide refused to accompany me to the voodoo grounds, or the *candomblé* house of life, as it is known. She has a real terror of the conjure women. Females act as intermediaries with the gods in their religion, brought from Africa on the slave ships. I did not press her. She will be my assurance of rescue if there is danger.

Thus I found myself being led through the darkened streets by a young black girl who has promised me that her peoples' magic will restore my errant royal lover to me. It is ridiculous, of course, but I have nothing to lose. In this country strange things happen. As we crept along, I recalled that Dom Pedro believed in all manner of African superstitions. He had a black herbalist who supplied him with goat's beard sedge, "to raise the prick" he had explained to me.

I was almost suffocating beneath a heavy, black cloak as we passed the slaves' church of Our Lady of the Rosary and eventually reached a clearing on the edge of the city. I knew we were near the sea as I could hear the crash of the waves. The slaves had set up an illegal shelter in which to practise their rites. Perspiring heavily under the cloak, I heard the ecstatic chanting and singing and drumming, the clack of gourds and coconut shells and the wiry twanging of the *berimbau*.

Eufrasia hid me in a corner of the enclosure, where I watched the old women dressed in white like ancient brides, their wrinkled leathery faces transformed to resemble black angels. The women whirled and turned like windmills, arms outstretched, slowly at first, then faster and faster as they became possessed, shaking and falling in a trance-like state. "The *orishas*, the gods, are speaking through them," Eufrasia whispered.

We watched for what seemed like hours as the chanting and drumming grew louder. A cockerel was sacrificed by a man dressed in straw and feathers covered with many strings of beads. Blood flowed across a pagan altar. I cowered behind the slave girl, fascinated and horrified by turns. When the ceremony had ended, everyone ate and drank and socialised in a bizarre version of an English supper party. The slave stew known as *feijoada* was much in evidence; black beans and smoked sausage with the salted ears, snout, trotters and tail of the pig. Jugs of *cachaça* were liberally poured.

Eufrasia led me away to where one of the white-clad conjure women was throwing cowrie shells on the ground. "She is a diviner; she will tell you the truth." My story was whispered in her ear. The woman barely glanced at me as she threw the shells, muttering to herself.

"What does she say?" I asked.

Eufrasia shook her head, "the affair will not end well." I almost snorted into the smoky, humid night where cooking fires lit up the scene.

"Is that all she can tell us? We already know this." The woman muttered again and wandered off.

"She will give you something," Eufrasia said. "You must put it in his food and it will bind him to you. Do you have money for her?" The old woman returned and

142

I gave her some coins. She handed me some herbs in a palm leaf, then snatched them back and gave them to Eufrasia as if I could not be trusted. Men and women were wandering down to the beach, throwing things into the sea and singing.

"They are praising Iemanjá, the mother of the waters," my slave told me as we crept back through the night streets trying to avoid the militia men. When I fell into my bed, exhausted, I could hear the singing and the drums ringing in my ears. I showed the herbs to Adelaide next morning and she cried out, "No, madam, no!" She is right of course. I have no intention of using the herbs. I could not risk harming the heir to the throne. My very life depends on it. I gave the palm leaf's contents to Eufrasia and told her to throw them into the sea. She shrugged and took them without a word. As she walked away I called after her. "Why did you offer to help me?" She replied without looking back, "Because you threw the whip away."

With a sudden change of heart I rushed after the slave girl, breathlessly calling her to return the package. "I will keep the herbs. They may be useful in the future." Wordlessly, she handed them to me. My maid shrugged her shoulders with an "on your head be it" expression.

Adelaide returned to packing our belongings. Dona Serafina came to the house and watched silently as I kissed little Sebastian for the last time. I wonder if I will ever see him again. Perhaps we will meet again one day in Europe. He would be grown up and I will be a stranger to him. I stood at the window until the litter carried by the royal slaves disappeared along the street.

"It is for the best," were Dona Serafina's parting words, and of course she was right.

CHAPTER
EIGHTEEN

January 3rd, 1819

Mr and Mrs Luccombe are coming to escort me to a farewell dinner tonight. They have been loyal friends and the souls of discretion. I must talk to him about giving Eufrasia her freedom. Dom Pedro has given permission for this and has also promised that reports on my son's progress will be sent to me at intervals.

January 8th

My dinner with the Luccombes was a restrained affair. Although my friend tried to cheer me by saying how glad I would be to return to England after my unpleasant adventures, he sounded a trifle unconvincing. Eventually, after catching his wife's eye he subsided into an embarrassed silence.

I said very little, aware of the pitying looks directed at me by Mrs Luccombe. As the dessert was served I raised my eyes from the plate and we all three chorused as one, "It is for the best." I gulped and felt my eyes filling with tears of mingled regret and relief. Mrs

Luccombe clucked over me while her husband stared out of the window. The household slaves pressed against the walls like black marble columns, gazing at us with blank eyes. Their ubiquitous presence was something I would not miss.

After I collected myself, we discussed the voyage to the West Indies where I must wait for another ship bound for England.

"The journey to Jamaica is not a long one, thank God," said Mr Luccombe, "and a stay of a few days there will be most pleasant. At least you will be on British soil again." His wife added that they had greatly enjoyed their stay on the island when they were en route to Brazil. I dreaded another sea voyage but I could hardly cross to the other side of the world overland. Hopefully, the voyage would be shorter and more bearable than the ghastly journey I had experienced from Europe to Brazil with Dona Leopoldina.

I bade a cordial farewell to my friends and returned to the house. Adelaide had completed the packing of our goods and there remained only the task of handing Eufrasia the document releasing her from slavery. I had requested it from the court and the prince had agreed. My former slave's inscrutable expression vanished for a moment. She covered her face and rocked backwards and forwards. I placed a purse of money in her hand.

"Thank you, Eufrasia, for everything you have done for me." The girl did not respond. She simply carried the paper, the purse, and her few belongings through the door. As she passed me she briefly passed her cool, blue-black hand over my cheek. Then she was gone.

"We should have asked her to take the parrot," Adelaide commented.

We boarded the ship a few days later. A court official came to see us depart — no doubt to make sure that we actually left. The prince sent a magnificent bouquet of vivid pink cattleya orchids to the quayside. There was a brief message, "*My fondest regards . . . always at your service.*" I clutched them to my bosom as, slowly, the ship sailed across the vast, magnificent Bay of Guanabara. My Brazilian adventure was over.

Part Two

CHAPTER
NINETEEN

February 6th

As I waited on the quayside in Falmouth, Jamaica, for a carriage to convey me to an inn, I noticed an elegantly dressed gentleman dismounting from a horse and engaging one of the sailors in conversation. After giving the man some instructions, he moved closer and doffed his hat to me.

"May I be of service to you, madam? I believe you are newly arrived on the island. I am Martin de Fontblanc Macaulay of La Nouvelle Heloise in the parish of Saint Catherine."

He regarded me with a twinkle in his brown eyes and a decidedly forward manner. He wore a red hibiscus flower on the lapel of his coat and his dark hair was as carefully arranged as that of any member of the *ton* in London. This man had designs upon my person. When a lady travels alone she must be on her guard.

I bowed my head and thanked him, saying that I was awaiting conveyance to an inn. The gentleman clapped his hand and summoned a servant, almost from the air, who was commanded to carry our baggage while Mr Macaulay offered to act as a mounted escort. The carriage duly arrived and Adelaide and I were transported away to our destination.

When we arrived at the inn, I thanked our escort warmly and he remarked that he hoped we would meet again during my stay.

"Do you know that gentleman?" I asked the innkeeper, who replied that Martin de Fontblanc Macaulay was a creole of French and Scottish descent, whose family moved to Jamaica from Martinique during the eighteenth century. Obviously everyone on the island knows the history of their fellow citizens.

"Mr Macaulay now owns a large sugar plantation with many slaves, following the death of his elder brother." Was I mistaken or was there a guarded tone to the innkeeper's words?

"Surely there are no slaves on this island anymore?" I exclaimed. "Have they not been emancipated?" The innkeeper gave a surly shrug and muttered something about "Johnny new-comers." The rest was inaudible.

Falmouth is a delightful town, full of newly-built houses in the style so popular at home. It is like a miniature Bath, but with sunshine and no disagreeable, decrepit people bathing in hot springs. The dockside was bustling with people, merchants and their many servants or slaves, with a large number of ships coming and going. The innkeeper told me in his scarcely intelligible accent that, "Falmouth is the jewel in Jamaica's crown. We send great wealth to the Mother Country."

February 8th

It was not long before my path crossed with Mr Macaulay's again. When I went to inquire about our ship to England, who should I find chatting amicably with the captain but our gallant escort?

"Indeed, sir, you are dogging my footsteps are you not?" I remarked in jest. He made me a low bow and assured me that our meeting was a happy coincidence. After the captain confirmed that the ship would not sail for another week, Mr Macaulay said it would be a pleasure to be able to show me his beautiful island.

"Will you do me the honour of dining at La Nouvelle Heloise this evening, madam? My brother and I would be delighted to receive an English lady." I could hardly refuse such an invitation, although we had not been officially introduced. It seems that manners are somewhat more relaxed in this part of the world.

The gentleman arrived in person to escort me to his home. "It is called La Nouvelle Heloise after my great grandmother, who came from France via Martinique. When the family moved to Jamaica, my great grandfather chose the name. You will, I am sure, appreciate the pun in the title?" I looked at him blankly for a moment, then smiled and nodded. I had not the faintest notion.

The house was charming; a large plantation mansion in pastel shades of blue and pink with delicately carved verandas and shutters. Acres of sugar growing land surrounded the house but I saw no one toiling in the fields that day, although there were black servants in the house.

I was introduced to Mr Macaulay's younger brother, James, who was a good deal taller than his sibling with a somewhat careworn air. He was responsible for the day-to-day running of the estate during his brother's absence, as Mr Macaulay was abroad for some years. He has been back on the island for several months, I gathered.

"But Jamaican life is not to my taste," he told me as we sat down to dinner in the elegant, if sparsely furnished dining room. "I left the West Indies to complete my education in England and then I joined the army to fight Napoleon. I fought at Waterloo, you know, like your late husband, dear lady." His gaze travelled boldly over my person, settling on my bosoms which had increased somewhat in size since I became a mother. I fluttered my eyelashes and adjusted my light Indian shawl.

"How did you come to be in Brazil, Mrs Wickham?"

"Indeed," I sighed. "After the sad loss of my husband it was the greatest good fortune that I was offered a post at the Portuguese Court in Rio, due to the efforts of an influential friend." That part, at least, was true.

"And how did you find life in Rio, madam?" asked Mr Macaulay, leaning even closer across the table.

"I can scarcely begin to tell you of my diverse experiences there," I cried, clasping my hands together. "Their way of life is so strange, so exotic and colourful, and their manners so different from those of the

154

English. I was quite overcome until I adjusted to their customs, and to the heat."

"Ah, yes, the heat," he remarked. "It is wearing for new-comers but I was raised here and it bothers me little. I confess I found the English climate very harsh but I greatly enjoyed the congenial society. The ladies especially were most gracious."

I could imagine the ladies welcoming this rich, handsome stranger. His appearance was far more pleasing than Dom Pedro's, although he is not tall. He congratulated me on mastering the Portuguese language to some degree. "It is an outlandish tongue, is it not?" He had fought in the peninsular campaign and knew Spain and Portugal quite well.

As the meal progressed, my companion confessed that he was thinking of returning "imminently" to England, leaving his younger brother once more in charge of the estate. "I need the stimulus of London or Paris. Life is so narrow and provincial here." Indeed, his description of society on the island made it sound very much like Meryton with sunshine. He leaned in again and patted my hand in a familiar manner.

"Too much quiet and ease can be stultifying, do you not agree, Mrs Wickham?"

I assured him that I was hoping for some peace and quiet after the excitement of Rio, "Although I fear the rigours of the sea crossing." I described the horrors of the journey to Brazil and he laughed.

"Do not expect a comfortable trip this time, but perhaps the boredom may be enlivened by an agreeable companion." I cannot comprehend his meaning.

We dined on river mullet and fried pork with many unusual greens which are grown on the island. There was the usual shrimp, beans and rice found everywhere in this region but I accepted only a little of this. I had vowed never to eat shrimp again after I left Brazil.

During the following week as I waited for the ship to England, Mr Macaulay frequently entertained me at his home and drove me around the island to glimpse the many beautiful sights. He described the island in great detail, saying that it had been a paradise for him when he was a child.

February 15th

Only a few days after our first dinner he called for me at the inn. We drove first to La Nouvelle Heloise where he proudly showed me the mangos which had been cultivated from the first seeds introduced to the island from India.

"The story is that a British man of war intercepted a French ship from the East Indies carrying these seeds. Their cargo was confiscated and the seeds brought here. Our mangos are the descendants of those first fruits." I smiled at his Jamaican use of language which is often old fashioned and quaint. The mangos, however, were magnificent.

A plate of them was set before us and as we bit into the delicious orange flesh our faces became soaked in juice. The scent of tropical fruit and jasmine flowers was heady on the veranda. I could have been back in

156

Brazil with Dom Pedro, but Mr Macaulay was at least easier to understand.

He leaned close to me, attempting to mop the juices from my bodice with a linen kerchief. We swayed towards each other, giggling and dripping juices. I had not felt so carefree in a long time.

Mr Macaulay suddenly put out his tongue and licked the side of my mouth before winking in a suggestive manner.

"La, you are bold, sir!" I cried as he once again attempted to mop my bodice. When we had recovered ourselves, he called for water so that we could wash off the stickiness. A servant offered a jug of lemonade and later we departed in a carriage toward Montego Bay. In the distance, I saw the figure of James standing in a field overseeing the work.

"He enjoys it," said Mr Macaulay.

As we drove, my host told me more about the island which he pronounced as Yamaca. "It is an Arawak word meaning a place of rivers and springs. The Arawaks were the first settlers here long ago. There are groups of them still but their numbers are dwindling. There are other groups too, especially in the Blue Mountains. We never go there."

"Why not?" I was intrigued.

"Because of the Maroons. They are former slaves who escaped from the Spanish when we assumed control of the island. They are very fierce, but the British made peace with them. They leave us alone and we leave them alone."

"The island appears to be full of mystery," I told him. He nodded.

"There are many different groups and nationalities here — Jews, Arawaks, English and Americans, even Scottish/French settlers!" He laughed and pointed the whip at himself.

CHAPTER
TWENTY

The week positively flew by as I was whisked around the island, being shown many of the beautiful vistas and magnificent rivers. Our longest journey was to a place north of the capital, Kingston. It was a small settlement known as St Thomas which was famous for its hot springs.

I gave a bitter laugh when my escort told me this. Had I not spent enough time in the city of Bath? I explained to Mr Macaulay that the words "hot springs" brought an image of broken down, unwashed people with unfortunate skin conditions. He laughed and said that St Thomas was very different.

When we reached the springs high up in the rocks we found a crowd of people, black and white of all types and classes — the rich man, the slave and the free. The black men bared shining bodies as the water gushed over them. Others were pummelled and massaged by men and women with sticks.

The white people stood apart while their servants brought pitchers of water to them. Many of the white people looked as if they wished they could also remove their clothes. We arranged ourselves on some flat rocks as if for a picnic, while Mr Macaulay called for water.

He poured a cup for me and I regarded it, dubiously recalling the sulphuric taste of Bath Spa water. "At least it does not smell of bad eggs," I remarked.

My escort urged me to drink. "There is nothing unpleasant in this water, Mrs Wickham. You have a treat in store." He downed a cup very quickly and poured another. I took a sip and then drank the cup down. It was a hot day and I was thirsty. My companion immediately poured me a second.

I felt a strange sensation creeping over my body, a tingling like pins and needles but very pleasant. I drank more water and began to feel extraordinarily at ease with myself and the world around me. Mr Macaulay beamed at me and we both began laughing immoderately and talking nonsense. The warm, loving feeling grew more intense and looking around I could see others in the same condition, smiling vaguely and drinking avidly.

"The water cures your physical ills and makes you feel good inside," intoned Mr Macaulay, as if quoting from the prayer book. He slurred his words a little and I giggled. "Yes, I feel almost regenerous." I meant regenerated but the word did not come out quite right.

People were moving into the little grass roofed cabins nearby. My escort took my arm and we followed them into an empty cabin. There we half lay, half sat on makeshift couches while wonderful sensations coursed around our bodies. We began to giggle helplessly, clutching each other for support. Mr Macaulay grasped me in his arms and buried his face in my hair, but I pushed him away and he collapsed on his couch laughing helplessly.

At that moment I was in love with the entire universe and everyone in it. I even felt benevolent toward Dom Pedro, his mother, and Mr Darcy. I even forgave Captain Lafitte for attempting to kidnap me. Never had the sky seemed bluer, the gushing water more crystal clear. God was in his heaven and I— Suddenly the feeling of well-being evaporated as the tingling sensations died away. I sat up feeling like my usual self, but at peace. Mr Macaulay's eyes were closed and I prodded him gently. Reluctantly, he sat up, brushed himself down and offered to fetch the picnic which we had left in the carriage.

As we began to eat I asked eagerly for more water. "It is such a hot day!" He laughed and shook his head at the longing in my voice.

"Too much of the magic water is not good, my dear. It should be used sparingly. The local people believe it is a gift from God and so they named the place after St Thomas the apostle."

"Do you think it is a gift from God?" I asked. He gave me a sly wink.

"It could equally well be a gift from the Devil. Perhaps I should take some back for James. He has need of it."

We ate our food and drank cordial in place of water before driving back to Falmouth over atrocious roads. The feeling of contentment was quite dissipated after being bounced over many miles.

Back at the inn, I told Adelaide about the magic water and she immediately became pettish because I had not thought to bring some for her to taste.

"It was probably spiked with gin," was her sour verdict. I was forced to mollify her with the gift of a fine, lace edged kerchief. I must keep her content. She knows too much.

"It will soon be time to embark for England," I reminded her. We both groaned at the prospect and I wished for a supply of the magic water to enliven the journey.

February 16th

There remained only one more dinner at La Nouvelle Heloise before I left the island. Mr Macaulay had courted me most assiduously and I was not surprised when he announced that he had booked a passage on the *Ocean Queen* which would convey us to England. He was trying to impress me and I was willing to be impressed, dear reader, for was I not once again alone and friendless, if not exactly penniless?

Before we left the island, I ventured to a jeweller's shop to sell my miniature of Dom Pedro. How could I explain to relatives in England how it came to be in my possession? I could not afford to be compromised. The jeweller found the piece "most interesting". I do not know if the fashion for lovers' eyes has reached Jamaica. They are somewhat behind the times. Nevertheless, I received what appeared to be a good price. Adelaide was charged with getting our baggage to the ship and safely stowed in our cabin.

As we embarked, Mr Macaulay held my arm saying, "May the winds be gentle. Are you acquainted with the operas of Herr Mozart, Mrs Wickham?" I confessed I was not. "The aria I quoted from is the most beautiful song of farewell I have ever heard." He looked soulfully at me and hummed a few bars. "Will you not call me Martin now that we are to travel together?" I smiled and lowered my eyes.

"I could not use such a disrespectful title, sir." Perhaps this is an example of colonial manners.

CHAPTER
TWENTY-ONE

February 17th

Mr Macaulay continues to pay court to me. As soon as I emerge from my cabin he materialises by my side, a dapper sprite with his extravagant West Indian mannerisms. When I recall his charming house and estate and his wish to live in England, I consider that I could do worse. However, this time I will settle for nothing less than a wedding ring. I could not in conscience return home a widow when such an opportunity presents itself.

You may judge, dear reader, that I am acting in haste in this matter. It is true that I am somewhat impetuous by nature, but I also feel a degree of desperation. I would be undone if news of my liaison with Dom Pedro and the birth of our child became known to my relatives in England. In short, I need a husband and Mr Macaulay appears to be eminently suitable.

Later that same day

Accordingly, it appears that we can accommodate each other. Mr Macaulay is in need of a wife and I am able to supply that need. Our bargain was sealed when he produced a flask of brandy mixed with some of the magic water brought from St Thomas. The hour passed most pleasantly.

Later still

I must confess that I was taken aback when that gentleman, within hours of his proposal and my acceptance, suggested that we should be married at once by the ship's captain. I had anticipated a ceremony in London or even at a port *en route* — the ship calls at Madeira and somewhere in Ireland, but my husband-to-be was insistent. He professed himself so eager for us to be united that he could wait no longer. Such enthusiasm is flattering, of course, but somewhat puzzling.

When he returned from a consultation with Captain Maguire, he told me that the captain was more than willing to officiate. His first mate and Adelaide would act as witnesses and he looked forward to drinking our health at a celebratory dinner tomorrow evening.

Twenty-four hours remain in which to contemplate my change of status. I was comforted by visions of Mr Macaulay's large estate, reflecting that the unfortunate Wickham had nothing to offer me on our marriage except the ten thousand pounds supplied by Mr. Darcy which was soon dissipated.

At last I would have a home, even if it was thousands of miles away. The prospect of living in the West Indies had little appeal but later, who knows? How impressed my relatives will be with my good fortune! No more penniless officers and lowly curates will be dangled before me. Mr Macaulay and my family know nothing of my adventures in Brazil and I shall take care to see that this state of affairs continues. I know I can rely on Adelaide's discretion, but I must keep her with me always and see that she is well rewarded.

February 18th

A rapid change of cabins has been arranged. My maid, somewhat surprised, will occupy Mr Macaulay's cabin and he will move into mine after the ceremony.

When I told her that I had nothing to hand except my well-worn blue silk gown she muttered her favourite mantra, that I was not lucky with gentlemen.

"But he is offering marriage!" She shrugged and I thought I heard the word "chancer." I chose to ignore this and threw a handsome shawl over my gown. I will wear my pearls for good luck.

February 28th

The following morning dawned clear and bright enough with a heavy swell. When we presented ourselves to the captain in his cabin, Mr Macaulay eyed my pearls approvingly. He is something of a connoisseur of jewellery, although he has offered me nothing except the wedding ring set with a small turquoise, which he says is a family heirloom from France.

The ceremony was brief and I suspect that the captain was not entirely sober, although it was only eleven of the clock. However, he is a sailor and an Irishman to boot. Afterwards, my husband swept me up in a tight embrace and Captain Maguire shook our hands vigorously before the ship gave a lurch which threw us against the cabin doors. Mr Macaulay pocketed the marriage document and escorted me back to our cabin where he insisted on consummating our nuptials, despite my protestations that it was almost lunchtime.

Conjugal relations at sea in a cramped, narrow berth are not recommended, especially when there is a heavy swell. After several uncomfortable preliminaries my husband gave up the attempt and re-arranged his clothes. Although handsome of face, he is slightly under average in height and slight in every other respect, I noted. Nevertheless, we will deal well enough together, I believe. Married life is not to be compared with the passionate flights of *les affaires du coeur*.

That night I managed to change into my lemon and white cut work gown and Mr Macaulay wore his best burgundy broadcloth coat. There was much drinking of toasts at the table and it was fortunate that the first mate is a sober individual, otherwise I cannot imagine who might have been fit to steer the ship. After imbibing a good deal of brandy my husband sank into his berth that night, giving me only a quick peck on the cheek and a pat on the rump. However, I am too accustomed to the ways of men to be affronted by his behaviour.

I enjoyed a fair night's sleep despite some snuffling and snorting from my spouse. And so I am now Mrs de Fontblanc Macaulay which has a satisfactory ring, and I am a respectable woman again. Let Mr Darcy dare to sneer! I recalled my meeting with another West Indian nabob at Pemberley before I left England, but I suspect that the Macaulay fortune is not in the same class.

A few days later the ship docked at Madeira, where we enjoyed a few days on shore while it was provisioned and more goods were taken on board. This constituted our honeymoon and we found the island very pleasant and floral. It is known as the island of eternal spring, full of flowers, fruit and sweet wine. We were able to explore a little in a small carriage drawn by mules.

It was with some reluctance that my husband was prevailed on to make me a gift of a piece of lace which is made exquisitely here. He claimed not to have more than a few coins on his person. Fortunately, I had enough in my purse for the purchase. I hope I have not married a miser.

I whiled away some time on the voyage deliberating on the kind of household we would set up when we arrive in England. We will, of course, live in London and I shall insist on two matching footmen and our own carriage. My husband is unwilling to discuss these details, becoming vague on the subject whenever it is raised.

He is very anxious to visit Pemberley and has taken it upon himself to dispatch a letter to my brother-in-law by a faster ship. I confess I do not look forward to meeting my relatives again after the manner of my leaving, but I accept that I must introduce my husband to the family.

Mr Macaulay spends a great deal of time in the evenings playing cards and drinking brandy with the captain while I occupy myself with a copy of *Melmoth the Wanderer*, which awaited me in Jamaica, sent by dear Selena. It is recently published and quite delightfully horrid.

March 9th

When the ship docked briefly in Ireland, Adelaide said she would throw herself overboard if we did not disembark and I must admit that I shared her feelings. If only I could be sure that this would be my last long sea voyage, but there was no such re-assurance available.

My husband is also eager to reach England. He speaks frequently of how much he looks forward to meeting the Darcys at Pemberley. I assume that, like the rest of the world, he is bedazzled by my brother-in-law's wealth and status. I have not yet informed him of Mr Darcy's antipathy toward me — and mine for him.

March 15th

Eventually, when the ship arrived in Liverpool, we were once again on terra firma, only to be shaken and jolted over country roads until we reached Derbyshire. I have surely aged a decade since I left Brazil. Adelaide must procure some Milk of Roses to recover my complexion as soon as possible.

My husband, however, was all sprightliness and bounding energy He grew visibly more excited as we entered the grounds at Pemberley and progressed up the long driveway.

"Magnificent! Magnificent!" he burbled, "such a splendid vista. I had not realised . . ." his voice trailed away almost reverently. Adelaide sniffed loudly and I raised my eyebrows.

CHAPTER
TWENTY-TWO

I held my breath as we stood in the entrance hall. My brother-in-law stood half way up the grand staircase looking down on us with an air of invincible superiority, aided by the supercilious portraits of his ancestors adorning the walls. Mr Macaulay and I looked up at him wordlessly. The spell was broken by Lizzie, who rushed forward to embrace us warmly. Mr Darcy descended the stairs reluctantly, I thought. He cast his eye over my spouse before shaking him by the hand. I was given the briefest of acknowledgements. The look in his eyes would have cast a chill over a Jamaican plantation.

I tried to recall how many miles and how many countries I had traversed since I last set foot in this house. What life-changing events I had endured, dear reader! My mind began to bend under the strain of remembrance. If my family had but the slightest idea that I had given birth to a royal child, almost been carried off by pirates, tossed on the high seas, married on the high seas, not to mention being lady-in-waiting to a princess, they would have been quite scandalised.

"Is that not so, my dear?" Mr Macaulay was saying.

"Oh, yes," I replied as Lizzie led me away.

After we had been shown to our room, I was called to admire Charles Fitzwilliam, the rapidly growing heir to Pemberley, together with his baby brother. I suffered a pang as I thought of my little Sebastian. How much had he changed since our parting?

When we joined the men for dinner, we found them deep in conversation. Mr Darcy was becoming animated on the subject of estate management while my husband recounted his experiences as a plantation owner, omitting to mention that his brother has carried the burden of the Macaulay acres for some time. My brother-in-law deigned to address me at this point if only in the third person.

"We, my wife and I, are delighted and relieved to see Lydia married." Surely the word relieved was unnecessary? My husband laughed and patted my hand.

"We are most happily settled, I thank you." Lizzie immediately wanted to know where we would live in England, "Unless you are intending to return to the West Indies soon?"

"No!" I gave an involuntary cry, adding, "we intend to live in London, do we not dearest?"

"Perhaps," my husband replied. I have had occasion to remark on this vagueness whenever the topic of our living arrangements is raised. "We have but lately arrived in England, madam, and we were anxious to introduce ourselves to you. We have made no firm plans as yet." I tightened my lips and considered kicking my spouse under the table.

Lizzie immediately said that we could remain at Pemberley for as long as we wished. "Do you not agree, dearest?" Darcy nodded, unsmiling. Mr Macaulay looked mightily relieved and thanked them effusively. I wondered again at his reluctance to spend money. There can be no worse fate for a wife than to be shackled to a miser.

When we retired that night I reproached him for his unwillingness to return to London and he became instantly irritable.

"For heaven's sake, madam, we have but this minute arrived. After all our travelling surely you will relish time to relax at this magnificent estate?" I felt a pout appearing. It is true that if Pemberley had been owned by anyone else it would have been delightful.

"I am not on the best of terms with Mr Darcy. There has been much ill will between us." My husband waved an arm to dismiss this.

"Surely that is all forgotten now that you are safely wed? He appears pleased and satisfied."

"We should travel on to Longbourn to visit my parents," I countered. "They will be expecting us." The prospect did not fill me with joy, but it was more agreeable than being under Mr Darcy's frigid gaze. My husband would not be moved. "In due course, in due course."

During our stay at Pemberley I do not recall my husband parting with any money at all. He even borrowed a few coins from me to give to the estate workers who assisted him when he was fishing or shooting. He accompanied Darcy on horseback around the estate for hours. I often found him contemplating the view from the windows as if the vast acres were his own.

Meanwhile, I was closeted with Lizzie and the children while she told me how happy I would be when I became a mother. Sometimes the burden of my secrets becomes unbearable and I shudder to think how I could be undone if Adelaide turned against me. My life was in the hands of my maid. What would Wickham say to that?

I have attempted to hide what remains of my former employer, Mrs Makepeace's, gold coins from my husband. A woman should always retain an air of mystery and these matters are best kept from one's spouse. Women have so little in this world and it is forfeit to one's husband upon marriage. I do not intend this to happen to me. The coins are kept in a locked trunk labelled as belonging to Adelaide. I withdraw money only when I am alone. What trust I am placing in my maid!

March 19th

When I told Mr Macaulay that I needed new winter clothes now that we are in England, he had the effrontery to suggest that I might borrow some from my sister. There is something very wrong here. I hope I have not made a dreadful mistake.

March 25th

As the days pass certain facts are becoming apparent to me. My husband is doing everything in his power to ingratiate himself with my brother-in-law. He is particularly anxious to know if any cottages are empty or available on the estate. Cottages? What can he have in mind — a new life as a gamekeeper with his wife taking in washing, perhaps? I am beginning to realise that Mr Macaulay is not all he seems.

"You are not lucky where gentleman are concerned, madam." Adelaide uttered those words a long time ago when I was involved with the count and several times since. I could only agree with her, but I have been powerless to alter my fortune or my inclinations.

Now, once again, I am embroiled with a man of dubious character. He is a gambler, as Wickham was, and just as unsuccessful. Like Wickham he gravitates towards Mr Darcy. I fear it will all end badly unless I can persuade him to set up home in London forthwith.

One evening before dinner I drew Mr Macaulay's attention to details in the London *Times* regarding desirable houses to rent in fashionable areas. I adopted my most persuasive tone;

"If we cannot purchase a property in town there is no shame in renting somewhere, at least for the duration of the season. We can also hire a carriage and engage staff when we arrive." My husband brushed the newspaper away in an irritable manner.

"Why do you wish to return to London?" His tone was petulant. "Can we not enjoy living in this magnificent house on this fine estate? What more can you want, my dear?" My patience was beginning to fray. I ground my teeth involuntarily — always a sign that I am sorely tried.

"Because I do not wish to be a supplicant at my brother-in-law's table forever. He has no liking for me and we are received on sufferance. Why are you so unwilling to set up home somewhere?" A dark thought occurred to me. "Is it because your credit is poor, sir?" At this point my husband threw the newspaper on to the floor and trampled on it furiously like a child who has broken a toy in a temper tantrum.

"Do not interfere, madam!" he cried. "I will decide our future plans. Your role as my wife is to be agreeable, something you appear to have little talent for."

I made one last attempt to be charitable and wifely by offering another suggestion that might improve our finances. I reminded him that I had written a novel in the Gothic style for which I had high hopes. It needed only an approach to the office of John Murray (dear Lord Byron's publisher). My husband snorted and glared at me, not quite simultaneously.

"I ventured to read some of that unremitting drivel, my dear. You carefully left the manuscript in various places for that purpose, no doubt. Any self-respecting publisher would light his cigars with it." He snorted again, then ducked as I picked up a small ceramic statue and prepared to hurl it at him.

He marched out of the room, leaving me to seethe with fury and to contemplate my worst fears. I am convinced that my husband's financial problems are worse than I had thought. Calling for pen and paper, I sat down to write a confiding letter to Selena.

If only we could arrange a gaming salon for a short time. In the past we had always kept ourselves in funds in this way. Then, of course, I did not have to answer to a husband but I sensed that Mr Macaulay would not object. He gravitates naturally towards games of chance. In addition, I still remained confident about my Romance. What did Mr Macaulay know of such things? He often said that he never read fiction.

After I had sent off the letter, Lizzie came to my room and a distressing half hour ensued while she again waxed lyrical on the joys of married life and the delights of motherhood. If only I could have told her about little Sebastian, who would surely be taking his first steps by now. All I could do was listen and nod in agreement. My sister noted my strained smile. Lizzie is no fool.

"Is everything well between you and your husband, Lydia?" she asked. "I hope you are not having regrets already." I sighed; it was a relief not to have to dissemble.

"I believe Mr Macaulay is keeping the truth from me. Our financial position is less rosy than he led me to believe. If I question him he becomes furious and stalks off." Lizzie looked worried and patted my arm in an attempt to be comforting.

"That would explain his interest in the estate and its properties. I think he would like to settle here."

"Yes," I replied, unable to keep the bitterness out of my voice, "especially if he could stay rent free." My sister looked puzzled.

"What of his estate in Jamaica, surely you could return there?" I explained that his brother ran La Nouvelle Heloise and neither of us were inclined to return to the West Indies. Lizzie sighed and rose to leave.

"I could speak to my husband if you wish, Lydia."

"No!" I almost shrieked. "You know how he regards me. If you wish to help, dear Lizzie, suggest to my brother-in-law that it is time we moved on to our own household. That will at least force my husband into action." She nodded and left the room while I contemplated an uncertain future once again.

Dinner table conversation was somewhat strained that evening. I knew that Lizzie would have spoken to Mr Darcy about our dilemma. She is not one to shirk her responsibilities. Having agreed to my suggestion, she would have acted quickly. My husband was unusually subdued. He was still annoyed because I had pressured him about our living arrangements. Darcy was his accustomed taciturn self except when Lizzie smiled at him, when he softened visibly. How fortunate was my sister — a wealthy, loving husband, beautiful children — everything a woman could wish for. I, in contrast, had a feckless, improvident husband and a lost child.

"The fault, dear Brutus, is not in our stars, but in ourselves . . ." That was one of the few Shakespearian quotations I could recall and how aptly it described my own shortcomings.

At this point my husband abruptly excused himself from the table and withdrew. He returned moments

178

later with dilated pupils and a disturbing glitter in his eyes. His taciturn manner changed abruptly, becoming hectic and garrulous with much unnecessary laughter. Darcy looked at him in amazement as my husband began to praise the food extravagantly. It was "ambrosia, the food of the gods. Your cook is a paragon, a culinary angel, madam." Lizzie appeared slightly bewildered.

"I thank you, sir; Mrs Matthews does her best. We prefer plain English fare for the most part." Mr Macaulay giggled again and prodded a slice of pork before knocking over his wine glass. As a red stain spread over the white cloth, a servant rushed up to assist.

My husband leapt from his seat waving his arms and laughing like a hyena. His arm caught the unfortunate footman a blow across the face that almost felled him. Darcy sprang up to intervene and the three men became entwined in the strangest manner, Mr Mac laughing uproariously the entire time. When order was restored, Lizzie hastily suggested that we retire.

When the men re-joined us later my husband had quietened somewhat but began to giggle again when Lizzie attempted a tune on the pianoforte. Alarmed, I took his arm and led him away. "My husband is unwell," I announced. "Please excuse us."

When we reached our bedchamber he turned to face me. I could tell that something was amiss. His face was very pale and his nostrils were distended in an alarming manner.

"So!" he exclaimed, "I think you have been conspiring with your sister, my dear. Can I not expect even a modicum of loyalty from my own wife? Must you thwart me at every turn?"

"I cannot imagine to what you are referring, dear husband," I replied uneasily. I had a very good idea.

My husband raised his voice. "Your brother-in-law is already suggesting that we have outstayed our welcome here," he fumed. I pointed out that we had spent some weeks in the house. "We were invited to stay indefinitely, as I recall," he replied.

"You know that such invitations are not to be taken literally. It is a matter of good manners."

"Apparently so, even when members of the family are involved." I begged him to tell me why he would not remove to London. "Because I have no money!" he hissed. The truth at last.

I fled from the room and found Adelaide waiting in the anteroom. "I cannot imagine why my husband is behaving so oddly," I exclaimed. Adelaide gave me a wry look.

"He has been using the white powder, madam."

"White powder?" Realisation slowly dawned. I put my head in my hands for a moment. "He said it was Jamaican powdered coconut — his favourite sweet." Adelaide sighed and rolled her eyes. I returned to our room where I found Mr Macaulay slumped in a chair looking vacant. I prodded his arm sharply but there was no response. A few moments later he burst into tears and threw himself onto the bed. At that moment I recollected that powdered coconut is not usually snorted like snuff. I retired to sleep in Adelaide's bed while she sat up in the anteroom.

CHAPTER
TWENTY-THREE

The following morning, I returned doggedly to the question of our finances. My husband appeared to have recovered from his encounter with the white powder.

"So, are you telling me that you have nothing?" I asked, resisting an urge to laugh. Surely he could not be serious. Mr Macaulay refused to meet my eye, preferring to fiddle with his snuff box.

"Of course, I have an estate as you well know. It is just that . . ."

"What?"

"It is heavily mortgaged."

"And why is that?" But I already knew the answer. Fate has decreed that I should always marry a gambler, although never a successful one.

"I have a lack of ready cash," he continued, "and more bills to pay. I thought you might be able to help me, my dear." A wheedling note entered his voice which I ignored.

"Then there is no possibility of our setting up home in London in an appropriate style?" He looked anxious and a little shamefaced.

"Not at the moment, but in time. I had thought to ask your brother-in-law for some assistance."

"Darcy?" I shrieked with laughter, "so that is the way the land lies. Did you marry me because of him? Then you are an even bigger fool than I thought. I have nothing of my own except a few hundred from my parents and some jewels. I am detested by my brother-in-law who has tried his best to be rid of me on many occasions and who now thinks you have obliged him. He would never give us a penny." Of course Mr Darcy had given me an allowance to stay away from Pemberley but I did not intend to mention that.

My husband threw his snuff box down and left the room, his face a mask of fury.

He disappeared for several hours that morning after telling our hosts that he had urgent business in Derby. Mr Darcy was somewhat surprised but loaned him a good horse for the journey. It was not until I began to dress for dinner that I realised something was amiss.

"Where is your jewellery, madam?" Adelaide asked. "The box is empty." I seized it from her, shook it and turned it upside down. Nothing emerged. I sat as if turned to stone while Adelaide, as always, voiced the unthinkable. "Mr Mac 'as gone off with your jewels, madam." Noting my expression in the mirror she added, "I was just about to fetch a dish of tea," before escaping rapidly from the room.

I do not recall how I passed the next few hours. My husband did not return for dinner and if any conversation passed between the remaining three of us I have forgotten it. All I can remember is that I ground my teeth so hard I almost sustained lock jaw.

After retiring early to bed, pleading a headache, I occupied myself in devising suitable punishments for my spouse; boiling in oil was the favourite.

How foolish I had been to show off my jewels to that man. Naturally, I did not mention how I had acquired the Prince Regent's necklace. I said that the Princess of Wales had given it to me for "services rendered." My husband had accepted this as he had accepted that the pearls and diamond brooch had been left to me by a grateful employer. That at least was correct, and had I not earned them in my tedious role as companion to an elderly lady in boring Bath?

Eventually I drifted into an uneasy slumber and I awoke alone next morning. Mr Macaulay did not return until after breakfast, rather the worse for wear. When he appeared in my chamber he informed me casually that he had, indeed, removed my jewels.

"You have done what? Are you saying that you have sold them, my diamond collar, everything?" I could hear my voice beginning to crack. "What kind of blackguard have I wed? Those jewels were all I had in the world." It was true, dear reader, I had already made large inroads into the three thousand pounds left to me by my previous employer in England, Mrs Makepeace. I emitted loud sobs of fury as I began throwing anything that came to hand in the direction of my spouse.

He dodged the various objects and said in an injured tone, "It was my right as your husband — and you have brought no fortune of your own to the marriage."

"No!" I screamed, hurling a vase which shattered against the door, "and neither have you. Your estate, the house, all mortgaged to pay your gambling debts. What a fool you are, and what a fool I am." We glared at each other in mutual loathing, knowing that we had each contracted a marriage for financial gain and we had both been deceived.

Mr Macaulay collapsed onto the floor with his coat tails spread around him, the picture of sulky disappointment, like a five-year-old who has been told there will not be any jam for tea. Meanwhile, I leapt and quivered in front of him, beside myself with fury.

"What have you done with the money?" I screeched.

"Paid off most of my debts, of course. And I did not sell your pearls or the gold locket."

"That was because I was wearing them!" I screamed so loudly that Adelaide rushed in with a cry of, "Madam, I thought you was being murdered." Behind her I could see a group of servants in the corridor listening in fascinated suspense for the outcome of our argument.

"Leave us," my husband told her, "your mistress is merely assaulting me in her customary manner." He turned to me. "You really must control your propensity for violence, my dear." Adelaide made no move to leave the room.

184

"Mr and Mrs Darcy are returning from their drive, madam," she told me and I was grateful for the warning note in her voice. I collapsed onto the bed as my husband prised himself off the floor.

"Well, my dear, we must make the best of things. I am of a philosophical nature. We will have to seek our fortune in another country if we cannot rely on the generosity of your brother-in-law." I goggled at him hearing only the words "another country."

"I will not return to the West Indies," I snarled.

"The matter is already in hand. I obtained a commission in the East India company army, as a precaution. We leave for Calcutta within the month." I heard a low moan of pain reverberate around the room and I realised it was coming from my mouth. My husband beat a hasty retreat and Adelaide pressed herself against the closed door.

"Don't take on madam."

I waved a limp arm at her, "Laudanum!" I croaked. She nodded and left the room.

It was ever thus, dear reader. My disastrous taste in men had again been my undoing. I was now shackled to a second wastrel of a husband, with a taste for gambling but not the wit to profit from it. Furthermore, it appeared that I would be forced to embark on another long sea voyage to another distant land. Surely, no Englishwoman ever had such misfortune? I had not yet been sentenced to exile in Van Diemen's Land, but no doubt that would happen in due course. Who would save me? Why had I not married a curate? If only I was Spanish or French —

then I could withdraw into a convent and end my days in peace.

At this point Adelaide returned with the laudanum bottle. She administered a few drops and I collapsed gratefully onto the bed and waited for oblivion.

CHAPTER
TWENTY-FOUR

As if the loss of my jewels was not a sufficient blow, I faced another humiliating experience caused by my inept, meddling husband. When I emerged from my laudanum induced haze and ventured downstairs, I heard raised voices issuing from the library. Lizzie appeared with her finger pressed to her lips and the tips of her ears red with anxiety.

"What is happening?" I asked. Somehow I knew that whatever it was, I would be the cause.

"Your husband is arguing with mine. The subject appears to be money." Or the lack of it, I told myself. Had I not warned Mr Macaulay about the folly of asking Darcy for money? Naturally, he had chosen to ignore my advice and no doubt I would pay the price.

At that moment my husband threw open the library doors and erupted into the hall where he leaned against a wall for support, breathing heavily. He was followed by my brother-in-law, the picture of cold disdain. His eye fixed on me as I tried to remain unobtrusive in the lee of my sister.

"So, madam," he boomed. "I might have deduced that you would marry another scoundrel like the first, one who would eventually come begging for money and assistance, having frittered away any fortune he might once have possessed." Darcy paused for breath and Lizzie valiantly intervened.

"In fairness, dear heart, I do not think that Lydia knew anything of her husband's financial affairs. She cannot be blamed for them."

"No, indeed," I added. "When I met Mr Macaulay, he was a respected plantation owner. How was I to know that he had gambled everything away? I thought I had finally made a good match and that my family would approve of me at last." I gave a soft sob at this point to gain sympathy, but only Lizzie was impressed. My husband shot me a poisonous look as he pawed the walls for some kind of assistance. Mr Darcy's stony stare remained in place. I could have reminded him that he had expressed pleasure at my union with Mr Macaulay, but that would not have served for the moment.

"You have a taste for gamblers and wastrels, Lydia," he said. "It has been your undoing, despite our attempts to advise you." I could not deny the justice of this remark. I wriggled with embarrassment when I recalled the triumphal tone of my last letter to him before I left Pemberley for the continent. He turned to my husband.

"You, sir, are a scoundrel and no gentleman. You will get nothing from me. You must both sink or swim by your own efforts."

Mr Macaulay greeted this announcement with fury and I thought that he would assault Darcy, but Lizzie bravely stepped between them and managed to quieten things. Her husband retreated to his library and my spouse rushed out of the front door as if pursued by demons. I assumed he had been using the white powder again.

When he reappeared after some days, it transpired he had been finalising our departure for India. His appeal to Darcy for funds was intended to be a last attempt to avoid the need for emigration. At least he could not sell any more of my jewels. I intend to wear my pearls day and night. Adelaide suggested that she should bury them somewhere in the grounds but I rejected this idea. Suppose we forgot where they had been placed?

Now my mind was solely occupied with plans to leave the country, although not for another far-off, tropical destination. I would gladly return to Paris, preferably without my husband. At a pinch I could endure his company, but I will not forgive him for the loss of my jewels. I had not even worn the diamond collar in public. How admirable it would have looked when promenading in the Place des Vosges. However, this was no time to be planning my wardrobe. Adelaide, who was hovering nearby read my thoughts again. It is frightening how easily she manages this.

"Perhaps you could slip away to your friends, madam. I mean when Mr Macaulay isn't about." Yes, surely Selena and Miles would assist me. We could resume our former carefree life of card parties and *joie de vivre* once my husband was on the high seas. How I missed those days which, from my present position, seemed so happy and uncomplicated. I turned to my maid.

"I doubt you are keen to accompany me to India, Adelaide?" She sighed and looked despondent.

"Is the climate like Brazil?"

"At the very least . . . if not worse. I believe there are many precious jewels to be found there — and elephants. That is all I can say with certainty."

She sighed again. "I had better start the packing."

Later, she informed me that my "tropical muslins" as she called them, were in a sad state. They had accompanied me to Brazil and the West Indies and were now little better than limp rags. An entire new wardrobe was required and it was unlikely to be supplied from my husband's pocket.

When the Darcys were told of our proposed departure for India, he gave a snort of disbelief and Lizzie became agitated on my behalf.

"Must you go so far . . . and to such a wild place? Surely it would be preferable to return to the West Indies?" I began to weep at this point while my brother-in-law sneered and said that he doubted we would go farther than Longbourn where my husband would try to ingratiate himself for a lengthy period of time. "Or perhaps he will press his suit with your sister Jane and her husband."

Mr Macaulay could be seen pacing up and down on the terrace at that moment, looking morose. No doubt he was pondering on where his next supply of white powder could be obtained.

Lizzie urged her husband to be more charitable. Indicating my distressed self, she informed him that Macaulay had sold my jewellery to pay his debts and I was more to be pitied than blamed. I wept louder at this and Mr Darcy threw up his hands. "I cannot suggest anything more. Your sister has made her choice and must abide by it." He left the room leaving the two of us in a dejected heap on the sofa.

"He thinks I should have married a curate, no doubt," I said sniffing loudly. My sister gave me a speaking look. I twisted my handkerchief viciously and declared that nothing would induce me to go to India. "Make no mistake, I shall escape one way or another."

"But as his wife you must accompany him," Lizzie admonished me. "What would become of you alone here?" What indeed? I knew I could not expect help from any member of my family but if I could join forces once again with my friends . . . I needed to make plans.

When I returned to my room I found that Adelaide had anticipated my decision. She had packed a few essential items assuming, as she put it, that "we would make a run for it." I instructed her to pack my manuscript. I had not mentioned its existence to my sister, knowing how little regard she has for my accomplishments. Lizzie is such a blue stocking. How surprised she will be when it is published.

"How will we leave here unobserved, madam?" Adelaide asked. I thought for a moment. "First I must send a letter to my friends at Stoke Newington. Then all I need is a distraction. Mr and Mrs Darcy are giving a grand ball in a few days. There will be so many people present. We can slip away and borrow some horses. My sister Jane and her husband are invited. We can take their mounts. My sister will surely not pursue me as a thief."

Adelaide looked doubtful, but continued packing.

April 3rd

The following days were difficult ones. We all tried to avoid each other's presence, but we were forced to dine together. The atmosphere was strained. Mr Darcy uttered scarcely a word and even Lizzie eventually gave up trying to make conversation. Mr Macaulay appeared deeply depressed which I took to mean that his supply of white powder was exhausted.

On the day of the ball my husband's spirits appeared to improve. No doubt, he hoped to induce some of the guests to play at cards. That would suit my plans very well.

When my sister Jane and her husband, Charles Bingley, arrived they greeted us warmly. Obviously Mr Darcy has not had time to inform them of the situation. I had donned my best gown of lilac satin together with Mrs Makepeace's pearls and endeavoured to put on a brave face for the first part of the evening, taking time to talk with my sister, catching up with news and gossip. Jane and her husband have not yet been blessed with children, which saddens her and she commiserated with me on my own barren state. What a fraud I have become.

I discovered to my annoyance that, in addition to his other shortcomings, my husband was a poor dancer.

192

After a few clodhopping attempts he retired to the card tables, and I was grateful to Mr Bingley for leading me out in a most gallant manner. I essayed one or more dances with gentlemen to whom I had been introduced and I would have deemed it a most pleasant evening had I not been planning my escape.

At about eleven of the clock, after refreshments were served, I slipped away unobserved. Adelaide was waiting with my cloak and, clutching a small grip, we made our way to the stables where I convinced the stable boy to saddle up my sister's horses. We intended to ride to the nearest town where we would take the stage towards London. Once again I was fleeing from Pemberley like a thief in the night. Would it always be so? My life had come full circle and my problems remained just as insoluble.

CHAPTER
TWENTY-FIVE

April 5th

We arrived safely in London and made our way immediately to Stoke Newington. Miles and Selena had barely received news of my intended visit, but they welcomed me warmly and we were soon relaying titbits of news and describing our adventures during the last two years. My news was, as always, somewhat circumscribed. Selena exclaimed with delight as I described Brazil and its sights and sounds. Miles was impressed by my sojourn at the royal court, but did not envy me the long sea voyages. As a soldier he had no time for seafaring. My description of Mr Macaulay brought forth laughter and expressions of sympathy. If they disapproved of my flight from my husband they were too polite to say.

After an uncomfortable night — on a makeshift bed in Adelaide's case, and a couch in mine — it became apparent that we could not remain long at the cottage. There was barely room for two people and certainly not for four.

"I have a little money left," I told my friends. "We could take a house in London or, better yet, Paris and give some card parties as we did before." Miles looked embarrassed and Selena looked as if she had swallowed something sour.

"We cannot leave here, Lydia," she told me. "The salary Miles earns is all we have to sustain us, apart from his army pittance. This cottage is loaned to us free of charge as long as Miles is employed by the estate." I could not believe my ears. Had my friends lost all spirit of adventure in the years I had been away? It would appear so. "But we could make so much more money with the cards," I cried. "We have always been successful in that regard." Miles shook his head.

"Times are changing, Lydia. We cannot go on forever taking risks and living by the skin of our teeth. We are growing older and we need some security." Selena nodded vehemently and I observed that her general demeanour had indeed changed. Even her gown appeared more matronly in style.

Nothing more was said on the subject and we finished our breakfast in silence. I thought furiously as I drank my chocolate. There was nothing to be done; I must find Captain Marshfield again and ask for another assignment. I thought of my time in Italy with the count and the Princess of Wales. How long ago that seemed. I had no doubt that the captain was back in England and I resolved to call upon him as soon as possible. He had mentioned that his home was in Swallow Street. It would not be difficult to discover the house.

Adelaide and I duly departed on the stage for London the following morning. Miles and Selena bade me a fond farewell, begging me not to bear any ill will toward them because of their reluctance to join me, and declaring their undying friendship. In truth I could not blame them. I would probably have done the same in their position.

In London we put up at the Bell Savage Inn at Fleet Street and took a hackney carriage to Swallow Street. After various inquiries of tradespeople, I knocked at the door of number twelve. I had barely touched the door when it opened quickly and the captain emerged in full dress uniform as if about to attend a royal parade. He regarded me with astonishment for a moment and then laughed.

"No doubt you are here to make your report, Mrs Wickham. We have been expecting you." This was such obvious nonsense that I did not dignify it with a response. It pleased me a little that the know-all captain had not discovered I was now Mrs Macaulay.

"It is essential that I speak to you in private, captain. We have some matters to settle."

The captain invited me to return later that day, as he was off to attend a military parade in honour of the king's birthday. Adelaide and I were obliged to return to the inn and twiddle our fingers for a few hours as I did not dare attempt to visit the shops for fear of losing what little capital remained to me. We ordered a lunch of lamb chops and eventually returned to Swallow Street.

Captain Marshfield, now at home and sporting a magnificent purple and gold morning coat, welcomed me and proffered a glass of Madeira which I accepted gratefully. Adelaide retreated to the kitchen to gossip with the servants.

"Now tell me everything about your adventures since we last met." I gulped with terror at the thought but eyed him defiantly.

"I am surprised that you do not know more about them than I."

"I know that you travelled to Brazil with the Austrian princess," he replied. "I received some details from Luccombe." Was there a hint of a smirk on his face? It was not easy to tell with Marshfield.

"You did not know about my marriage, I presume? Apparently, you are not omniscient. I am now Mrs Macaulay." He look puzzled.

"Then why are you here? The presence of your husband would make it unnecessary and unsuitable for you to continue in our service."

I wondered if our dear monarch would know or care about my unsuitability. Reluctantly, I gave him my reasons for being in London without dwelling too much on my financial and marital problems. He gave a loud guffaw and slapped the arms of his chair.

"Truly you are the most unwise female I have ever encountered. Nevertheless, you have rendered some useful service." I was not greatly diverted.

"Nevertheless," he continued, "we cannot employ a runaway wife. Where had you planned to go?"

"Paris!" I wailed. "Please send me there." He shook his head but when I told him about Mr Macaulay's planned enlistment for India he perked up immediately.

"India, you say? Tell me more." I explained that as my husband had rendered us penniless by his feckless ways and that Mr Darcy had refused to help us, the East India Company army was his only option. The captain nodded, looking delighted.

"Now there is a place where you could be of some assistance. There is a great deal happening with the East India Company and the government needs to know about it. We also need to know more about the native rulers and their intentions. The company is seldom forthcoming about these matters. Your special gifts would be useful." I did not like his implications at all.

"My husband and I detest each other and I cannot face another sojourn in a tropical clime, not to mention another long sea voyage." Marshfield threw up his hands indicating that he could not help me. He gave me a promissory note for my expenses which still remained unpaid. This involved a trip to a bank. Adelaide was eagerly anticipating her wages which had not been paid for some months.

As Adelaide and I waited to receive the money I considered my options which were all too few. I knew no one in Paris who would give me a roof over my head. My money would last for a year if I lived parsimoniously. If only dear Mrs Makepeace was still with us. I could happily be her companion again in that wonderful city.

Selena and Miles were unable to help me and I could not set up a gaming salon alone. Also I had noticed that London's society was more sober than I remembered from a few years ago. Times were indeed changing. I could not return to Longbourn or Pemberley as a runaway wife. Perhaps I could impose on my sister Jane's good nature, but for how long? When I thought of the diamond collar that was to have been my security for life, my fury at Mr Macaulay brought a rush of blood to my head.

"Madam, your neck and ears are bright red," Adelaide commented. Men were staring at this highly flushed female so I calmed myself with an effort. When the money was given to me I sat clutching it and staring into the abyss. I sighed and turned to Adelaide.

"It will have to be India, I fear."

She nodded. "I know, madam."

I could hear Mr Darcy telling me that I had made my bed and I must lie on it.

CHAPTER
TWENTY-SIX

When we returned to the inn at Fleet Street, another unpleasant surprise awaited me. I found Mr Macaulay ensconced in the dining room gnawing on a chicken leg and drinking a tankard of ale like a common tradesman. His companion was a similarly dishevelled character from whom he appeared to have won money.

I stood riveted with horror but my husband greeted me amiably enough and introduced his companion who staggered to his feet and attempted a bow. I ignored him and addressed myself to my spouse.

"How did you find me?"

He shrugged.

"I did not find you, my love, because I was not looking for you. It was pure coincidence that I discovered you were staying here. I came to London to finalise affairs with the East India Company. This gentleman," he indicated his companion, "has recently returned from India and was telling me of his experiences." I shuddered. I did not for one moment believe him. He had deliberately tracked me down. The stable lad at Pemberley had directed him, no doubt. I should have offered the boy a larger bribe.

When the fellow departed my husband became less cordial, demanding to know why I had run off. "To escape from you," I told him. He laughed and seized another chicken leg, calling for fruit and tossing me a peach as if I were a monkey. My fury increased when I noticed an elegant new gilt snuff box on the table that looked to be of value. No doubt he had purchased it with the money from my jewels.

"I assume that your friends could not or would not assist you — or did your parents throw you out?" he asked with a sneer. I was aghast at his effrontery. He waved his tankard at me and drank to our success in India, "As I assume you will now be accompanying me." I bowed my head and he laughed again.

"You know I am completely indifferent to you," I told him. He agreed and said that he felt the same way toward me, but it would have been embarrassing to explain my absence to the Company.

If only women had choices in life. Why had I not left for the continent and joined a convent? I knew the answer. I must choose life, whatever the consequences.

I was obliged to take my husband to Longbourn to make our farewells where he ingratiated himself in his usual cynical manner. At least he did not try to borrow money from Papa. It was obvious even to him that my father had none. I could scarcely contain myself when my mother and sisters demanded tales of my time in Brazil. When will I see baby Sebastian again? When, if ever, will I see England again?

My usual healthy appetite had deserted me due to my melancholic state. As I toyed with a fricassee of rabbit at the dinner table, under mama's watchful eye, I imagined myself back in Paraty for a moment. I thought fondly of the guava paste made by Eufrasia on one occasion. It was, I explained to my family, a pink, firm sauce that was excellent as an accompaniment to cold meats or cheese. When paired with cheese the Brazilians called it Romeo and Juliet.

"They serve a gallimaufry of meats and fruits," I explained.

This explanation was received with blank looks from the family and one of my husband's high-pitched laughs. My sister Mary, naturally, demanded an intricate explanation for the name, which I refused to give. I retired to my room and wept in solitude.

When we returned to London I occupied myself in buying new clothes for the tropics, taking care to keep my money away from Mr Macaulay. The weather was dull and overcast and he declared himself anxious for some sunshine. No reference was ever made to his Jamaican home. I wondered how his brother was coping with the mortgaged estate.

April 19th

Eventually, the dreadful day dawned when we would embark. Adelaide and I were pale and drooping at the prospect. I had sent a note to Captain Marshfield and received instructions that I should wait to be contacted by someone in India. I would be paid the usual small fee but at least it would be mine. I would rather buy an

202

elephant than allow my husband to lay hands on the money.

"You never know, madam, there are diamonds in India too." Adelaide's optimism had resurfaced but I could not share it. Only that morning I had received a polite but firm letter from the publisher, John Murray, declining to publish my Gothic romance. The gods were indeed showing their displeasure. Nevertheless, I resolved to take the manuscript to India. Perhaps in the future I might publish it privately. Naturally, I did not add to my husband's pleasure by giving him this news.

CHAPTER
TWENTY-SEVEN

I stared up at the huge black and gold hulk that was the *Repulse* as it wallowed in the sinister green waters of the East India docks. The ship was well named. Everything about a long sea voyage repulsed me and I was again facing a journey of four to six months, after being on land for only a matter of weeks. We would round the Cape of Good Hope in this vessel. My heart sank into my boots. My husband had no such qualms. He gazed with admiration at the ship.

"Look at that beauty! See the guns on it? A great East Indiaman, a lord of the ocean." I said nothing. "The captain is an agreeable fellow, Woodward by name. I had some conversation with him earlier."

"Does he resemble Captain Maguire?" I recalled the Irish officer on our journey from Jamaica. "Ah, Maguire," replied Mr Macaulay. "He proved to be something of a villain. It seems that his papers were not in order. He should not have been in charge of a ship. I had it from Captain Woodward who knew all about the affair." I turned and faced him.

"Do you know this for a fact?"

"Yes, it is absolutely true. I believe Maguire faced severe penalties." Bile rose in my throat. I addressed my erstwhile spouse.

"You must realise that if Maguire was not authorised to sail the ship he was not authorised to conduct a marriage? That means we are not lawfully wed!"

Mr Macaulay took my arm and moved towards the gangplank. "Do not worry, my dear, nobody will know unless we tell them."

I gave him a shove that almost toppled him over the jetty. "What are you doing, woman?" he gasped as he tried to right himself. "Are you trying to kill me?" I refrained from answering that question. The answer was too obvious.

"My jewels!" I hissed. "If you are not my husband then you had no right to sell them. You are a thief, sir!" Mr Macaulay dusted himself off and again attempted to drag me up the gangplank. "Do not embarrass yourself, my dear. We are going to India because we have no choice in the matter. Come!"

CHAPTER
TWENTY-EIGHT

April 22nd

My Dearest Selena,

Since I informed you of my husband's dastardly behaviour regarding my jewels, and our imminent departure for India, you will have wondered how I fared. I regret to tell you that even greater tribulations have overtaken me.

You may recall that Mr Macaulay and I were married at sea by the ship's captain during our voyage from the West Indies. As I was reluctantly about to board the ship for India, my husband told me that the captain who performed the marriage was not empowered to do so — his papers were not in order. In short, we were not legally wed!

My consternation was bottomless. My body gave off effusions of rage, especially when I recalled the loss of my jewels which he had removed and sold. Mr Macaulay appeared unmoved by my reproaches, telling me that we had no alternative. Indeed, he almost dragged me on board. He had spent the money obtained from the jewels and we would have no way to sustain ourselves, Mr Darcy having once again cast me off.

It pains me to admit this, dear friend, but I have undertaken a voyage to the Indies in the company of a man who is not my husband. Naturally, I know I can rely on your discretion in this matter. All would be lost if this became common knowledge.

I will write again when we reach our destination. You may be sure that I shall find a way to improve my lot and to be revenged on Mr Macaulay. In the meantime we must keep up the pretence of matrimony.

Pray do not forget to send me a copy of Mary Shelley's *Frankenstein* when it is published.

I remain your dear friend,

Lydia Bennet Wickham (Macaulay manqué)

Part Three

CHAPTER
TWENTY-NINE

June 2nd, 1820

Mr Macaulay's faith in the "great East Indiaman" would, alas, prove to be misplaced. But more of that later. Having been almost dragged up the gangway onto the *Repulse*, we found that a mishap had occurred with our booking and no berths were reserved in our name. There was a good deal of damnation and blastings from Mr M, but we were forced to spend another two days in London before embarking on the *Tanjore* which was bound for Southern India with two companies of Lancers on board. The less said about *them* the better.

I am now imprisoned on this wooden hulk with only the close company of my wretched non-spouse, two disagreeable missionaries and their insipid wives. Thank heavens for Adelaide! Apart from a distant sighting of the Azores we will not see land until almost the end of the voyage, and we will have to round Cape Horn with its terrible storms where the ship will, no doubt, be torn apart like matchwood and we will all sleep with the mermaids.

"Don't take on so, madam!" Adelaide, loyal Adelaide, is on hand as always to offer cheery words.

Indeed, what would I do without her? She warns me whenever Mr Macaulay hoves into view so that I may avoid him as far as possible. The loss of my jewels causes me so much heartburn that I must needs resort to our dwindling supply of camomile tea. Water is, of course, strictly rationed. Even Adelaide has occasional fits of depression.

"Will we ever spend time on dry land again, madam?" she asks me. "I mean a long time — more than a year or two?" I wish I could offer her some assurance on this subject but my future is full of nothing but question marks. All I can promise is that if I ever acquire some of India's fabled jewels we will return immediately to Paris, permanently. *She* would prefer London, naturally, but Paris is good enough for *me*, I can tell you!

My maid's woeful expression remained unchanged. "What happens if you are only given an elephant or two instead of jewels?" she asked.

"No doubt those beasts are very valuable and could be sold for a good price," I told her without much conviction. Elephants may be as common as monkeys in that country for all I know. Mr Macaulay has told me that elephants are the chief mode of travel in India — although the officers have horses (naturally).

"We will be lucky to cover fifteen miles in a day with the beasts, plus the camels and baggage trains." He takes some pleasure in painting as bleak a picture as possible of our future life. Accustomed as he is to the intense heat of the West Indies, he has no fears on that account. Sometimes, when we are alone, he runs around on deck tearing at his clothes in mock affliction and yelling, "the heat, the heat!" Adelaide and I do our best to ignore him.

Fortunately, he spends a great deal of time playing cards with the military personnel on the ship. Frequently he loses, and he will then have recourse to the brandy bottle. As I no longer have any jewels for him to steal, I worry little. I still have Mrs Makepeace's pearls and I wear them day and night. Short of mounting an attack on my person he cannot remove them. I keep a heavy glass bottle at my side when I sleep, so that I may ward off a surprise ambush. Adelaide keeps watch and Mr Macaulay is usually too drunk to be any danger.

June 15th

Last night I had the misfortune to be seated at dinner next to Mrs Amelia Morrison, wife of the Reverend Morrison, one of the two Methodist missionaries. The woman has no style whatever and her muslins are a disgrace. She regaled me with descriptions of their plans to convert the heathen natives causing me to feel a sudden rush of sympathy for the said natives. Mrs Morrison eyed my pearls covetously, remarking on the fact that I wear them constantly.

"No doubt they are very valuable," she remarked. I sensed that this was a rhetorical question, and gave her an insincere smile. She leaned forward to her husband across the table and remarked that, "Mrs Macaulay's pearls would furnish a goodly number of mission posts for the heathen natives." I was so outraged by this appalling lack of manners that I almost choked.

Mr Macaulay chimed in with a leer, "It would be a great act of Christian charity, my dear." Overcome by fury, I told the assembled table that I kept the pearls on my person because my husband was a gambler. He is not my husband, anyway, but I did not wish that to become common knowledge.

There was an embarrassed hush for a moment while Mr M laughed the whole thing off and the other missionary, Mr Beck, tactfully asked me if I was interested in the history and geography of India.

"I led a society for the encouragement of the subject in my last parish," he explained.

Mr Macaulay remarked through gritted teeth, "Indeed, my wife was a keen member of our local histrionics society!" Mr Beck look bemused and I assured him that while I knew little about India, I was greatly fascinated by Roman history and the Ancients in general. Mr Beck said that, in his opinion, the Romans were somewhat too exciting and disturbing for the female sex.

"Oh, the gorier the better for her," Macaulay continued. "My wife would have lived on the Aventine hill in another life."

And I would have had *you* thrown to the lions, I thought. At this point Mrs Morrison pressed a small volume of her husband's sermons into my hands and I thrust it into my reticule intending to throw it overboard at the earliest opportunity.

On our departure, the channel was very rough and most passengers suffered from *mal de mer*. As Adelaide and I had long ago acquired our sea-legs we decided to remain in our cabins until the unpleasantness on deck was over. One cannot promenade on the quarterdeck without stepping over recumbent soldiers. There is, however, a military band on board and I hope to cavort a little with some of the officers later on. There is precious little entertainment otherwise. The Methodists will disapprove, I dare say. I shall contrive to be as happy as a bird with one wing. In the meantime I am reading Mary Shelley's *Frankenstein* again which is deliciously horrid and transports me completely from this wretched ship.

Once past the Needles, we bade farewell to the shores of England and eventually the sea became calmer. The *Tanjore* is a fairly new ship and the cabins are in far better condition than we have experienced on previous voyages. My whole world has once again shrunk to this twelve feet by eight feet space. When I think of the spacious halls of Pemberley I declare I could even endure Mr Darcy's company for an indefinite period.

CHAPTER
THIRTY

July 25th

As the days followed each other with nothing to do except observe whether the wind was in the right direction, whether a storm was due, would we be tossed around like ninepins and so on and so on, I resorted to playing games of draughts and backgammon with some of the officers. Adelaide, I noticed, is becoming very friendly with one or two of the bandsmen, despite the fact that many of them have their wives with them.

"Well, I do like a good tune, madam," was her excuse. As we passed the Azores we saw the rocky islands protruding from the ocean, wreathed in white fluffy clouds. A pod of dolphins was spied alongside the ship, where they leaped and tumbled for a good while, to everyone's delight.

Mr Beck, who is a good soul, if dull as ditch water, has offered to teach me some words in Hindustani. He says this will be useful to me and I could not disagree. Adelaide is learning with us. She has always had a facility for languages although she cannot read well. The weather is growing very warm and I am much bothered by prickly heat, an uncomfortable rash that I remember well from our days in Brazil.

It is now the end of July and although we have been at the mercy of a contrary wind for two weeks, we will soon cross the equatorial line where we will receive a visit from King Neptune and Amphitrite. The glimpses of the Southern Cross and the sight of the flying fishes playing around the ship lighten our hearts.

July 30th

We — the officers and ladies — assembled on the quarterdeck yesterday to await the arrival of the sea god as we anticipated the merriest event of the voyage. Together with the other ladies, I had donated an item of clothing to adorn Amphitrite, the sea king's spouse, who is to be portrayed by the largest, most muscular and unattractive member of the crew. The royal couple arrived on a gun carriage drawn by several half-naked seamen representing tritons.

Neptune was naked from the waist up and wore a pasteboard crown. He carried an offering of salted fish and a dead sea-bird as well as an ear trumpet. The procession included the Royal Baby, another large crew member with a greased belly; the ship's doctor; the barber with his razor; and someone dressed as a "sea bear".

The band played *Rule Britannia* and *God Save the King* as a rope was laid across the deck to represent the Line. The unfortunate male passengers and crewmen who had not previously crossed the line were shaven and dressed in ridiculous costumes before all manner of indignities were inflicted on them, followed by a dousing in sea water. Ladies were fortunately excused, although Mr Macaulay and I were introduced to King Neptune and bowed before him.

At the end of the ceremonies we were all doused with water by the fire engine and four hundred people amused themselves by throwing sea water over each other. We all gave a donation to Neptune before he left and in the evening the band played, we danced, and the sailors sang songs before splicing the mainbrace (that is to say, drinking grog). The celebrations continued into the early hours, but Mrs Morrison was taken to her cabin early by her husband, who did not approve of "pagan practices".

I made haste to write about these events on the following day, having slept late after the excitement of the ceremony.

August 25th

Some of the passengers have been shooting numerous sea birds, including albatross. One of the crew told me that shooting these huge creatures was considered bad luck and we might have cause to regret it. I remembered the poem by Samuel Taylor Coleridge that we had learned in the schoolroom, and I grew very uneasy.

When we rounded Cape Horn the gales were terrifying and the sea rose in awful grandeur, the waves as high as mountains. One of the Lancers was lost overboard and we all thought we would join him, but somehow we survived. A member of the crew was killed by a falling spar and there was a solemn service as he was buried at sea.

October 10th

We are now in the Doldrums, becalmed for almost three weeks. Water is now very scarce and the heat unbearable. Those who have the energy can dance quadrilles on deck because the sea is so calm. Having been confident that my last hour had come at Cape Horn I am now likely to die of boredom. Never has the prospect of a life as a curate's wife seemed more attractive.

Diary entries written in India
October 29th

My boredom was soon to be relieved, dear reader, in the most appalling way. The ship had put in to one of the Nicobar Islands to take on much needed water. Later, we were off the coast of Ceylon when the terrible mishap took place. Some spirit — brandy, no doubt — had leaked from a dislodged barrel in the hold. When a seaman inspected the barrels his candle fell from his hand and ignited the patch of liquid. The fire instantly spread through the hold and took the ship.

We were hurried to the lifeboats, unable to rescue any of our belongings and wearing only our morning clothes, and in some instances our nightwear. There was surprisingly little panic and thankfully no loss of life. I was frozen with terror for an instant and then the instinct for self-preservation came to the fore. Mr Macaulay seized me and almost hurled me at a crew member, who dropped me unceremoniously into the lifeboat. Adelaide followed in the same style. Mr M did not join us but was accommodated in another boat.

The boats reached the shores of Ceylon where local people came down to help us on the beaches. We found ourselves in a wild and lonely spot on the edge of the jungle with a few giant beehive houses strung on poles for the native people, surrounded by tall coconut palms. The locals indicated with much gesticulation that there was a mission post not far off. We made a fearsome trek through the jungle for a short distance before reaching this place. Thank goodness for the brave British Lancers! They supported and often carried us through the terrifying vegetation that reminded me immediately of my time in Brazil.

The native men were also familiar in their appearance, in that they were almost naked, their handsome brown bodies glistening in the sun. I noticed that Mrs Morrison could not take her eyes off them unless her husband looked her way. The mission station did its best for us but it was a small, simple place that could not cope with so many people.

We were surrounded by locals who offered us tropical fruit and coconuts, fish and small black pigs costing sixpence. As we had no money with us, complicated bargaining ensued. Mrs Makepeace's pearls were still attached to my neck but I noted that the natives were not interested in them.

"Pearls are plentiful enough around here," the local missionary told me. "They are much more interested in brass rings." Indeed, the locals and some of the soldiers who could swim had tried to salvage as much as possible from the wreck. The village headman brandished aloft some brass curtain rings triumphantly. Some of the Lancers sold their brass uniform buttons in exchange for food.

CHAPTER
THIRTY-ONE

November 10th

The headman of the village now proudly wears his brass buttons around his neck on a string. Adelaide was able to bargain with one of the local women for a length of blue cloth, which she wore sari style over her tattered petticoats. With the addition of some silver wire ornaments she looked quite *a la mode* in a savage kind of way.

My situation was little better although I had managed to cling to my shawl to cover my bedraggled cotton gown. I urged Mr Macaulay to do something about my appearance.

"I know you have some tobacco, which is greatly prized by the natives," I told him. "Can you not bargain for some cloth for me? I cannot travel on to India looking like this." He eyed my pearls speculatively as if wondering what use he could make of them, but I shook my head slowly and bared my teeth! He nodded and walked away along the beach.

Later he returned with a length of cloth and a few coconuts which he obligingly cracked open. I drank the refreshing milk gratefully while Mr M added some rum to his portion. I have no doubt that if he landed on the moon the wretched man would find some alcohol somewhere. He had purloined the rum from one of the barrels washed ashore from the wreck.

"The soldiers are making good use of them," he told me, "but it could be a devilish serious matter if the natives get hold of it. They are unaccustomed to alcohol and it could have a devastating effect."

And so, what more afflictions will beset us? Is it not enough that we are abandoned on a remote tropical island, clad in rags, barefoot and penniless, without the prospect of natives and soldiers running amok? I dread to think what could happen to us.

Adelaide does not seem too worried. She has already embraced island life, wandering along the beach barefoot in her new finery, eyeing the assembled male bodies. The soldiers have divested themselves of their uniforms because of the heat and are almost as naked as the natives.

"Madam, don't you think it could be a pleasant spot in which to spend some time?" she asked. "The locals bring us food, we don't need no clothes worth speaking of . . ." She did not need to add that a supply of rum and soldiers to while away the time added to her pleasure. Some of the band members have rescued their instruments and impromptu dances are held by moonlight on the beach, much appreciated by the natives who add their own version of dancing to the general merriment.

I cannot share her pleasure in this Robinson Crusoe existence. The presence of my non-spouse, the prickly-heat rash and my fear of the tropical vegetation and wildlife have ruined any appreciation I might have had.

The Reverend Morrison fears a total breakdown of morality if we remain here for any length of time. A message has been sent to the authorities on the island and we expect a rescue ship in due course. I am mortified at the thought of arriving in India in this condition. Will I be forced to sell my pearls . . . surely not all of them? It is outside of intolerable!

"Come and dance, madam," said Adelaide. "Don't take on so." I was not greatly diverted.

I have to admit that our diet, at least, has been much improved since we arrived on the island. After the miserable ship's rations and lack of water and fresh fruit we are enjoying tropical fruits, coconuts and roast piglet while the soldiers have rigged up fishing rods and can supply us with fresh fish. The natives refuse to fish for us. I believe this is because we are running out of items to use as barter. The local missionary told us that it was fortunate that we were shipwrecked on the Nicobar Islands. If we had suffered the mishap on the Andaman Islands not far away, it could have been very different.

"They are cannibals," he remarked.

November 16th

A ship has been sighted on the horizon and we believe it to be the rescue vessel sent to convey us on to India.

What relief! The officers are rounding up the men who are forced to don their uniforms, now stiff and unpleasant from a dousing in salt water. Whatever has been salvaged from the *Tanjore* has been assembled on the beach. I was saddened to find the remains of my copy of *Frankenstein* among the debris — but what joy! Mr Macaulay has found one of our trunks. Perhaps the man has some uses after all. A few of my belongings are in the trunk and I will not have to appear looking like a gypsy ragamuffin when we reach our destination.

November 17th

We embarked on the *Maid of Kent* where we were received with great kindness by the captain and crew who commiserated with us about our misfortunes. The Reverend Morrison was seen to fall on his knees on deck offering thanks to the Almighty for our deliverance. Adelaide watched with disgust. She is not religiously inclined and found no objections to island life. She is less than sanguine about India and I share her anxiety. It was fortunate that a ship returning to England with a light load was able to turn around and rescue us.

The rest of the voyage was fairly smooth. The Andamans were sighted in the distance and flying fish followed us once more. Finally we anchored off the sands of India before taking a boat up the Hooghly River. This is a great river and gave us our first insight into the vast land we had entered. We watched fishermen wreathed in white linen against the early morning chill when we anchored overnight on the second day.

On the third day we arrived at Chandpor Ghat in Calcutta. We had reached our destination after five months of travel. I was happy to be able to wear a respectable muslin gown to enter the city of palaces, as it is known. I no longer had a bonnet but I draped a stole over my head. Some appropriate apparel was found for Adelaide so that we did not appear too bizarre. Temporary accommodation has been found for us until we depart up country to Mr Macaulay's posting.

CHAPTER
THIRTY-TWO

December 7th

We are billeted for a short while in a district called
Chowringhee which is very pleasant and full of fine
houses occupied mainly by Europeans. The houses have
large windows and matting on the floors to keep the
place cool. I was surprised to find that the rents are
very high and the large number of servants deemed
necessary are also a great expense. We will not be here
for any great length of time, however, and I suppose the
rents are being paid by the Company, else Mr M is
using the money gained from the sale of my jewels.

A native called a sirdar is in charge of the servants.
He reports to me every morning with paper and reed
pen in hand awaiting my orders. He is a lean, dark,
elegant man wearing a spotless white turban wound
from many yards of muslin. His beaded leather slippers
are much coveted by Adelaide. During our conversa-
tions the sirdar uses many extravagant expressions such
as, "You are my sun, moon and stars, memsahib,"
which I find somewhat embarrassing, but it is the
custom here apparently.

As in Rio it is possible to obtain all manner of European goods — fine china, furniture and glassware — at very high prices. All the servants and merchants demand something called *dasturi* — a gratuity for any service carried out or purchase made.

Many of the Company staff and their wives have generously loaned us clothes and goods after hearing of our predicament. I have been able to obtain a silk gown in which to appear at the Governor's ball. These are held frequently and if we stayed here for any length of time we would be financially ruined, if we are not so already. I have no doubt that Mr M's gambling debts on the ship were large.

Adelaide is something of a curiosity here. Few of the ladies have brought their own maid owing to the number of servants available, but she was accustomed to this situation in Brazil. Her presence is vital to me because the native servants are very lazy. They will perform only certain duties — often only one — because of their religious customs which are extremely complicated. Then they promptly go to sleep. We must take account of their unaccountable practices — Hindu, Muslim or Sikh — which must not be violated at any cost.

The climate is very uncertain, oven-hot one week, followed by strong breezes and heavy rain. The houses have a wonderful contraption called a *punkah* which is a giant wooden fan operated by ropes and pulleys. The operator is called a *punkah-wallah*.

The other Europeans call us griffins. All newcomers are griffins for their first year in India. Once again I am suffering as I suffered in Brazil from lassitude caused by the heat, mosquito bites and all the problems of a tropical climate. My ringlets hang in damp, bedraggled strands — and my hair was always my best feature!

My head aches when I try to remember the strict rules governing the Hindu caste system, not to mention other religions. Muslims will not touch a plate on which pork has been served; all things relating to the cow are sacred to Hindus, as well as monkeys and many other animals. Adelaide is quick to pick up all this knowledge. She has been to the bazaar and already has a print of the elephant-headed god Ganesh pinned up in her room. "On account of he brings good fortune and luck," she told me. I can imagine what the Reverend Morrison would say to that.

We will certainly have need of luck. We are due to leave in a few days to travel hundreds of miles upcountry to the desert state of Rajputana, to the station where Mr M must join his regiment. Meanwhile we must appreciate the comforts of home as they exist here: iced claret, sausages in tins, pots of soup sent from England, custards and arrowroot puddings prepared by Adelaide to offset the consumption of curry. I am growing quite fond of this spicy dish but the consequences can be unfortunate. There is gentleman's relish for Mr M and cases of marmalade and other necessities of life.

In the absence of Mr M and other Europeans I have succumbed to an unseemly vice. I have acquired a *hookah*, an oriental pipe machine, and I smoke apple tobacco and rosewater in private. I know this is a shocking pastime for a lady, although it is very popular with the men. However, I find it soothing and a distraction from the heat and the wildlife and the problems of my future. Mr M thinks I have purchased it as a gift for *him*.

December 24th

He mellowed sufficiently to make me an accidentally generous gift. He purchased one of the Calcutta lottery tickets on my behalf, as a Christmas gift, and I became a winner. The prize was 5,000 rupees and Mr M immediately bought two fine Arab horses with the money. Graciously, he has given one to me, a beautiful grey with a good temperament. I have christened it Byron after my hero. I have also adopted a small terrier called Fudge, left by a departing official. I try to keep him to the veranda — with some difficulty — lest he come to harm. He is a sweet thing and a charming companion. Sometimes, when I am alone with my pet and smoking the *hookah*, I feel almost content with my life.

December 28th

I ventured out yesterday with Adelaide and a servant as bodyguard to visit some of the sights, exposing myself to the sounds and smells of this incredible country. Many of the sights are terrible; diseases such as elephantiasis (which causes the limbs to swell to monstrous size) and leprosy are very prevalent. The beggars, including small children, are often grotesquely deformed on purpose to extract money from passers-by. The wildlife is as shocking as it was in Brazil: the monstrous spiders, the small lizards constantly darting across the walls! Worst of all, very large rats are everywhere and the servants who sleep in the lower part of the house are constantly being bitten.

Compensation comes from the exotic jewellery, often made from beaten silver and semi-precious jewels which can be purchased for very little money. Adelaide has already had henna designs applied to her feet in the native manner but I forbade her from applying them to her hands. Secretly, I would like to try this custom myself, but it would outrage public opinion. Everywhere there are snake charmers and *fakirs* whose naked bodies are smeared with ash and mud.

These men are considered holy and often sit for years with an arm upraised until it becomes numb and withered. They mutilate themselves in gross ways to gain favour with their deities.

CHAPTER
THIRTY-THREE

January 5th, 1821

Our tin-lined trunks — the few we possess — are packed and we depart in two days. A new year and a new adventure.

Although we have been here only two months the servants are making a great deal of fuss, prostrating themselves and wailing as if we were their closest relatives. Everything is extreme in India, the climate, the food, the habitat and the emotions. This is part of its charm but it can also be very wearing to the Anglo temperament. In Adelaide's words, I wish they wouldn't take on so. Mr M has been forced to make large disbursements of rupees to them.

We are taking the horses with us although I do not know how they will fare on the journey. Indeed, I do not know if any of us will deal well with this situation, but we must join the cavalcade of soldiers, families, baggage carriers and animals, including camels and elephants. Fudge is, of course, travelling with me.

I have seen very few elephants as yet but I saw one of them in a procession painted and bedizened like one of the nautch girl dancers and wearing jewelled velvet cloths. The elephant did not appear to object to these adornments and carried its princely master respectfully. Its giant toenails were painted scarlet and its trunk gilded and painted in bright blues and greens.

I pray that the company will be large enough to keep off the wild animals that might attack us. There are tigers out there and one of the officers told me that one can hear the discreet coughing of leopards in the hills at dusk. I remember hearing from one of our servants that her child had been eaten by a hyena. Oh woe!

Adelaide, Fudge and I shall travel part of the time in a closed kind of litter drawn by bullocks and at other times I will ride Byron. Mr M spent our last night watching a fight between a snake and a mongoose. He watched from the veranda as the servants gathered around the men bringing the creatures. These events are greatly enjoyed by the natives but I declined to join him and retired to my room to check on the supplies of eau de cologne. I feel I shall have great need of it.

January 20th

Dust . . . dust . . . nothing but great clouds of pink dust; we are enveloped in it on the roads. I soon gave up the litter in favour of riding, after being tossed around in the greatest discomfort. The dust settles into a grey film that covers our clothing — my riding habit, bonnet and veils. It is in our eyes and mouths and nostrils but it appears not to affect the natives very much. We have not been troubled by any wandering bands of thugs, although I do not think they generally dare to attack Europeans.

My diary entries will be few during our journey owing to the difficulty of writing anywhere at all.

March 15th

When we reached Benares, where we will stay for a few days, I was forced to leave my lovely Byron with an English officer. The rest of the journey will be accomplished on a small, wiry, native polo pony that is much better suited to the terrain.

Benares is a very holy city for the Hindus, on the banks of the great Ganges River. My senses were assaulted by the hordes of pilgrims and families bringing their dead to the burning *"ghats"*, as they call them. It is considered very favourable to die or be burned here. You will go straight to Paradise, even if you are an unbeliever. The waters of Bath cannot make such claims, although I'm sure they would if circumstances permitted.

Fakirs or holy men are everywhere, a horrible sight covered in ashes and mud. There is even a sect which is believed to eat human flesh. It is outside of intolerable.

The city did, however, afford us a few days of rest and one incident redeemed the horrors I had witnessed. I was persuaded to rise at five in the morning and we took a boat out into the middle of the great river. Our guide threw orange marigold garlands into the river. Little candles in bowls bobbed in the water around the boat as the guide intoned a prayer. We watched as a great gold and orange sun rose on the horizon turning the waters rosy pink and gold. For a moment I could believe that this was indeed a stairway to heaven. India is full of both beauty and horror.

When we arrived on shore people were beginning to bring their dead to the burning places, smoke was rising and hundreds of people were coming to bathe in the sacred waters despite the presence of human and animal cadavers.

We have been somewhat refreshed by these few days and I was able to purchase some of the gold and silver tissue cloth for which Benares is famous, also some very stiff ribbon worked in silk and gold on which are the names of all the Hindu deities. The local people wear these around their necks. I decided to use this respite to send a letter to Selena.

March 18th, 1821

My Dear Selena,

You have not heard from me for many months and I am writing to assure you that I am alive and well, having endured many adventures, especially on our long sea voyage when we were shipwrecked! I wonder how many more misfortunes and adventures I must suffer? Already I have endured more of these in a few years than most people manage in a lifetime. When I consider that I will have spent no less than two years of my life at sea, should I live to make the return journey to Europe, it is outside of intolerable!

Our ship caught fire off the coast of Ceylon and we were able to reach the shore albeit with the loss of all our goods. We spent a few weeks as castaways with all manner of indignities and hardships, although I must admit that there were some compensations. Eventually a rescue ship arrived and we continued on to India in an even poorer state than we left England.

While we awaited a rescue ship we were obliged to live as best we could, bartering with the natives for food and scraps of cloth to cover ourselves. Some items were recovered from the ship, thankfully, one of our trunks together with many barrels of rum and brandy. As there were many soldiers on board you may imagine what use was made of these. There was a great deal of eating and drinking, dancing and singing.

The Edenic life has its good points but I confess I was overjoyed to be once again on board a ship. I did not think I would ever say such a thing! Not many days after we finally arrived at Calcutta. Would anyone in Meryton believe my stories? Certainly my family would scarcely credit it.

And so here I am in India at last: It is a vast country with many creeds and peoples.

I contrive to spend as little time with Mr Macaulay as possible. For appearances sake we must pretend to be man and wife but I am still full of rage at my situation and the loss of my jewels. I have acquired a beautiful horse called Byron and a pretty little terrier named Fudge and they are a great comfort to me. Loyal Adelaide is still with me. I must confess that I have taken up the vice of smoking (the hookah) in secret. I know this is despicable and unladylike but if I am not to deteriorate further I must have some comforts.

The Company people are for the most part very dull. Social life consists of endless balls when we are not travelling in great discomfort on elephants and other creatures. I anticipate an audience with one of the Indian princes who are festooned with jewels that they give out freely as gifts, if my friend is to be believed.

Needless to say I shall contrive to return to Europe somehow at the earliest opportunity. I am sadly lacking in reading matter, dear friend. If you could send me a novel or two I would be in your debt. I trust all is well with you and dear Miles? Please write and tell me all your news and news of what is happening in dear old England. I remain your forlorn and far flung friend,

Lydia Bennet Wickham (Macaulay manqué)

March 19th

We have now resumed our journey. Mr Macaulay was sufficiently jaunty to have importuned me last night but I refused him vehemently, reminding him that we were not *actually* married. This, together with a tirade about my missing jewels and other matters was enough to send him away in search of amusement elsewhere. He particularly enjoys watching the *nautch* girls and attending animal fights. No doubt he pursues other activities also which I prefer not to dwell upon. He took revenge by waking me in the early hours to describe an elephant fight he had witnessed.

"Do you know how they enrage the elephants to the point where they are willing to fight? They give them balls made of human ear wax to eat! Is that not remarkable, my dear?" I groaned and tried to fall asleep again, regretting the inevitable curry I had eaten the previous evening and its inescapable consequences.

CHAPTER
THIRTY-FOUR

March 31st

We are still on the road again plodding across country wearily towards distant Rajputana and its various kingdoms. For a while I rode alongside the wife of one of the senior officers. When we pitched our tents for the night Claudine invited me to her abode and told me some fascinating tales. She has been in India for two years and has met many of the native rulers. She showed me some wonderful jewels that were quite eye-popping in their splendour.

"The native rulers give us gifts when they meet us, for whatever purpose. It is the custom here," she said. I returned to my tent much cheered by this news. When I told Adelaide she looked hopeful, although as a servant she must expect to be content with a few silver bangles.

We rested during the heat of the day lying under the *peepul* tree, which is considered holy, or by mango groves and purple jacarandas. It is difficult to avoid one's prose becoming purple when writing of the colours of India: the violet sunsets, the lemon sky and the flaming orange dawns. The conversation among the

British is desultory at the best of times. Heat and weariness and the need to press on have jaded our appetites. I cannot face food and wish only to quench my thirst. Some of the officers can be vastly agreeable when they are civil and smart. Their wives are busy with small children or tending those who have fallen sick. Together with Adelaide I often feel I am on the fringes of this society. Mr M of course is definitely one of the merry band of soldiers.

How wonderful it will be to arrive in Delhi after such a journey. I fervently hope that we will be delayed there for many months before proceeding on to Rajputana. The Company is always very mysterious about troop movements. We are not likely to know anything until the last moment.

March 21st

Today an officer approached me when we were resting and Mr M was out of sight. He handed me a note from Captain Marshfield! The captain's arm reaches in to every corner of the world. He asked me to send a report on what I have observed of the Company's activities. I was extremely irritated. Does he imagine that I have the ear of the Governor, Lord Hastings, or that I am based in Delhi or Calcutta? Does he realise that I will be marooned in a remote desert garrison with only tiger hunting as a diversion?

I devoutly hope that some mishap will befall my non-husband so that I may return to Europe as soon as

possible. Perhaps not actually being eaten by a tiger —
I am not so hard-hearted. However, he could fall prey
to the cholera that has carried off so many of the troops
recently. (No doubt he is hoping for a similar fate to
befall me.)

The last phase of the journey to Delhi was the worst.
Everything conspired to annoy us. Hordes of monkeys
descended on us when we stopped to rest and eat.
Their little black paws would tear the food from our
hands causing the children to howl, but the native
troops care little. Monkeys are sacred to them. The god
Hanuman is a monkey so they are free to do what they
will. Mr M mutters about wanting a joint of lamb and a
dose of rhubarb while we reluctantly eat our chapattis.
The relentless heat is crushing.

April 20th

Our longed-for arrival in Delhi was of little comfort. We
were hastened on to Agra where our exhaustion was
forgotten for a while as we beheld the most beautiful
building in the world. It was a vision of white marble
radiance when observed by moonlight, huge, yet so
ethereal it could have been set down by a fairy hand.
The ingenuity of the architect and the builders lies
beyond mere skill. And to think that this loveliest of
buildings is a tomb, and a tribute to lost love!

Knowing that Shah Jehan had erected this tomb as a
memorial to his lost love, Mumtaz Mahal, brought
tears to my eyes. To be so beloved! Would I ever be so

241

cherished by any man that he would create any kind of monument to me, however humble? I felt a fit of the dismals threatening, combined with utter weariness. I had never felt so depressed as I stood weeping in the moonlight before such beauty. The darkness hid my tears and eventually I returned to our lodgings where there was great excitement among the womenfolk in our party. We had been invited to "breakfast" and an audience with the Maharajah of Jaipur.

There was a great deal of primping next morning and unpacking of creased gowns. Large amounts of eau de cologne were applied to jaded bodies and distressed ringlets. Adelaide unearthed a silk gown that had travelled fairly well and we set off for the palace escorted by the rulers' guards who were resplendent in gilded satin uniforms, far eclipsing our own finery.

When we entered the hall of audience I was overcome by the magnificence of pillared marble and crystal chandeliers. Inlaid mirror work and jewels winked from the walls in the morning sunlight.

The Maharajah was a small, elderly man with a white beard. He sat on a silver throne shielded by a canopy sewn with pearls and small rubies. Over his red brocade coat he wore a veritable breastplate of diamonds. His turban was secured with an extraordinary diamond peacock holding in its beak a rope of pearls and emeralds the size of quails' eggs. A gold tassel hung from this brooch, which is called a *surpeche*. It is anchored to the turban with a gold pin.

How could I ever have thought my three rows of pearls handsome? This prince was literally *cabled* in huge pearls and emeralds. We ladies sank down in deep curtsies and refreshments were served which I contrived not to eat. Then the *nautch* girls danced, also covered in jewels and gauze scarves. One or two of them were very beautiful but most were ugly. I noticed Mr M watching them avidly.

The ladies were presented with long strands of tiny pearl necklaces, which delighted me until I discovered that these gifts are seized by the Company. Sometimes we are allowed to buy them back. My friend Claudine had failed to mention this fact. She said the pearls were of poor quality. It is beyond irritating.

CHAPTER
THIRTY-FIVE

April 20th

When we reached Rajputana the women were in the fields or fetching water wearing their full-skirted fuschia and lemon costumes with long veils and tinkling anklets. As we rode past they drew their veils across their faces. Their turbaned menfolk were equally colourful, tapping their leather slippers with upturned toes as they sat by a well listening to a local musician playing the *sitar* and another playing the *tabla*.

April 30th

The great Fort of Rathambore is now within sight. I shall never complain again about a carriage journey from Longbourn to Pemberley. Having survived this trek with its discomforts, its frights, the fear of being eaten by wild animals I should be awarded a medal. Perhaps Captain Marshfield could arrange it. His shadow is never far away.

Rathambore is a great fortress many centuries old belonging to the Maharajah of Jaipur, who is now a

244

supporter of the British. Once inside the fortress we saw many palaces and temples including one to the little god Ganesh so favoured by Adelaide. Pilgrims come from all over India to this temple. There is also a temple to Lord Shiva.

The north side, known as the Palace of the Clouds, is largely in ruins but we have been given some rooms in the western half, which are quite bearable. Back in England people would consider our abode extremely primitive but we have already become accustomed to the strange mixture of the grandiose and the rustic. Most of the troops are accommodated in tents around the fort. The army is here to keep the peace since the treaty between the local rulers and the Company was only signed in 1818. There are still skirmishes between local princely armies from time to time.

Mr M is looking forward to a tiger hunt. "There are plenty of tigers in these parts," he said. The wildlife in general is very plentiful in this area, a fact that offers me little comfort. I must keep up the writing of this journal for posterity.

This land is part of the Maharajah's hunting grounds and, instead of the desert I expected to see, it is sited among hills and jungle and beautiful lakes. Mr M is growing more and more excited about this prime tiger country. He does not anticipate any fighting. The garrison is here to uphold the princely ruler's authority as a friend of the British, and to settle any tribal disputes. There are many Rajput clans and they have endless enmity with each other.

May 2nd

When we rode into the fort it was an extraordinary sight. Having just managed to learn the details of the Hindu religion I discovered that there is also an important temple to Lord Adinathji — a guru of the Jain religion which is akin to the Hindu faith. It is all too much for my tired brain to absorb. The site is quite picturesque with its archways and temples and ruins.

I was glad to collapse onto my *charpai* which I have become accustomed to on this journey. The swaying motion is most soothing and I fall asleep instantly. Tomorrow Adelaide must investigate the water supply, or lack of it. A chance to bathe has never seemed more enticing.

News has come that one of the Maharajah's most important officials will arrive in a few days. Perhaps he is the chamberlain or Prime Minister or something similar. His mission is to welcome us and to see that we are settled and lack for nothing. What irony! We lack for almost all the niceties of civilisation but my friend Claudine maintains that this posting is excellent because of the climate.

"It is not bleak desert or suffocatingly hot plains," she remarked. "There is cooler weather, there are lakes and trees. It is almost ideal — for India."

May 7th

When we heard that the official's procession was approaching the fort, everyone rushed to make

246

preparations. While the military did what they had to do, the ladies began elaborate rituals as we had for the Maharajah. Claudine told me she had heard rumours that the official — the chamberlain, as we knew him to be — was young and handsome, a great favourite of the ruler and extremely wealthy.

I hurriedly donned my best silk, added a lace fichu and, of course, the pearls that now seemed so meagre. Adelaide wove the string of small pearls that had been given in Agra into my hair. Fortunately, I had contrived to be unavailable when a Company official had asked for all the jewels to be handed over. Lastly, I emptied a phial of attar of roses onto my person. I had already noticed that Indian women — and men — valued perfume highly and used a great deal of it. Adelaide had obtained the phial during one of her excursions into the bazaar in Calcutta. Mr M was not there to comment on my appearance or my highly-scented self as I set off confidently to witness the chamberlain's arrival. Sadly, my hairstyle was somewhat obscured by my bonnet which is essential to keep off the sun's rays so I had to be content with bright new bonnet ribbons.

India had also put on its finest clothes that day. From our vantage point in the fort we looked down on palm-fringed lakes in the distance, lush green forests, valleys and crags all shining in the sunlight. Small domed pavilions could be seen amid the scenery and the cries of tropical birds and beasts could be heard in the distance until they were drowned out by the sound of horses with much jingling and shouting. The chamberlain is called Kymar Singh and his appearance at the head of his escort was incredible. I was overcome with admiration as I beheld his handsome figure with his jewelled turban flashing in the sunlight.

He wore a coat of sky-blue satin embroidered in silver; there were diamonds glinting in his ears and a diamond-studded sword hung at his waist. His dark, finely-drawn face wore the short beard brushed upwards with two points in the manner of the Rajput warriors. I was captivated by his brooding almond-shaped eyes and the almost vulpine expression in them. His horse was as finely caparisoned as its rider, and on the chamberlain's wrist sat a huge Sahin falcon on a jewelled leash.

I must confess, dear reader, that my heart missed a few beats at the sight of this wonderful man, if indeed he was a man, and not some god condescending to visit mere mortals for a few hours. Of course, he was not one of those Hindu gods with their animal heads and several arms, he was masculine perfection! My heart had not been afflicted in such a way since I first encountered my lost highwayman, now lording it in the jungles of Brazil with his harem. Indeed no European male, no British redcoat in his stiff uniform could compare with this vision.

The horsemen rode through the main gate, the garrison soldiers saluted and Kymar Singh descended from his horse. After receiving the greetings and salutations of the assembled company he invited everyone into the fort for refreshments. Our visitor had brought his own feast and his retainers immediately began to spread out various delicacies carried in muslin bags.

I scarcely recall the food served delicately on large green leaves. My senses were still reeling. The chamberlain had also brought a special drink to honour us. *Aska*, the traditional drink of princes, was offered to us in tiny cups set with precious stones. Claudine said this liquor was distilled from powdered jewels and fruits. We sipped it and became mellow and satisfied. I caught myself staring so hard at Kymar Singh that I felt sure he must be aware of the thoughts I was beaming in his direction. Once he looked at me, as I thought, and I gave him a dazzling smile.

Of course, it was pointless. I was not sitting close enough to him. I was the wife of a lowly officer, not important enough to sit with the honoured guest. Nevertheless, the chamberlain insisted on being presented to the ladies individually. We paraded past him dropping deep curtsies. He offered us the traditional gifts, tiny handfuls of emeralds and pearls with minuscule diamonds winking among them.

As I curtsied I contrived to lean close to this panther-like creature so that he absorbed the perfume of roses. I looked deep into his dark eyes and he returned a look that made me shudder inwardly. His arched black eyebrows met in a puzzled frown; a crimson circle between them that I knew to be a caste mark.

"Madam," he murmured, and I smiled invitingly. Then I was moving along making way for the next memsahib. When we returned to our quarters Mr M said I had "overdone" the perfume.

"There is no need to smell like a Sultan's harem," he remarked in his coarse manner. I ignored him. Fortunately, Adelaide had acquired a stock of oriental perfumes during her trips to the bazaar in Calcutta — sandalwood, jasmine, musk — as well as attar of roses and her hoard of silver bangles.

That night when Mr M was carousing with the officers I sat at the window in my room which was open to the stars. I smoked pensively on my *hookah*, occasionally nibbling at a sugared cinnamon curd cake that Adelaide had smuggled back from the feast. Fudge snored contentedly at my feet.

As I wondered how I could arrange a meeting with the god-like panther man, I remembered the soldier who had slipped the message from Captain Marshfield into my tent. I might prevail on him to arrange a secret rendezvous in the cause of discovering information to send to London. It was a feeble chance. There was no guarantee that the young officer would be able to gain the ear of such an important man — or that I had even caught the chamberlain's attention. But I was quietly confident.

CHAPTER
THIRTY-SIX

May 9th

My opportunity came the following afternoon. When we were resting during the heat of the day, I wrote a note for the officer which my faithful maid managed to deliver. She found him in the stables where he was checking on his horse, and after a little of the banter for which she is becoming renowned, she slipped the note to him.

Of course, Adelaide is a curiosity here, as she was in Calcutta. No other Englishwoman has a maid from home with her. There is a great deal of talk, and I even heard a rumour that she is thought to be my illegitimate sister.

While I waited impatiently for a reply from the captain's envoy I busied myself acquiring another horse with the money from the sale of poor Byron in Benares. I have called my new Arab steed Byron II and I plan to ride out into the surrounding country — although I will need an escort as bodyguard.

May 16th

The other wives now regard me as unwise, deeply eccentric and possibly scandalous. How they would revile me if they knew of the situation with Mr M! The tiresome Company official called today demanding the jewels we have been given. I managed to buy a few but the price was scandalous. As I gazed at the very small scattering of emeralds and pearls in the palm of my hand I realised that they would neither ensure my escape back to Europe nor provide a comfortable future.

May 18th

Today there is great excitement in the fort because letters have arrived from England. To my delight I found one from Selena as well as two letters from my family, sent by Lizzie and my mother. I opened Selena's letter in great excitement.

My Dearest Lydia,

What an age has passed since we last met in the little house at Stoke Newington. We read the dreadful news of your shipwreck but Miles made enquiries and we were overjoyed to learn that you were safe. What a dreadful experience! Indeed, my dear, you will have sufficient material for another Gothic novel before too long!

I trust you are safe and not too incommoded in that strange land. We hear that it is a most unhealthy place for Europeans.

We have some astonishing and welcome news for you. Do you remember that Miles' family has a small estate in Ireland? I did not expect that it would ever affect our lives in any way as there are others in direct line of inheritance. However, the ways of Providence are strange. We heard a few months ago that Miles' Uncle Ephraim had died of a sudden seizure. (He was over fond of the port bottle.) Only a few weeks later we heard that his heir had met with a fatal riding accident! The brother of the heir disappeared in Canada some time ago and has been officially pronounced dead.

Thus, Lydia, my dear Miles inherits! In fact, long before you receive this letter we will be installed in our new home near Drogheda. After so many misfortunes we are relieved beyond measure to be settled and I trust that you will soon be in the same position. When you are able to return home I hope you will visit us and stay for as long as you wish. With deep affection, I am,

Your friend Selena Caruthers

*Miles sends much love and good wishes.

What astounding news from my friends! I rejoiced in their good fortune and re-read the letter many times as several dull days passed in which I despaired of hearing from my panther god. I made a short expedition on horseback accompanied by a native soldier.

The forests were alive with chattering monkeys, shrieking mynah birds, tree mice and bandicoots, and all manner of exotic fauna that I am not yet able to identify. The emerald canopy stretched away to bare hills and glimpses of blue lakes. Little pavilions and solitary, vine-covered tombs called *chhatris* were dotted among the vegetation. My escort showed me India's largest Banyan tree located near the fort in enormous splendour.

It gave me a glimpse of an enchanted land until the heat grew too fierce and I returned to the fort. Lying in my *charpai* with Fudge in a room open to the elements and the mosquitoes, I reflected that the golden sun pouring into the room in the early morning was a great compensation. Adelaide has arranged some muslin over the windowless apertures. This reduces the midday glare but I fear it does not deter the mosquitoes.

Claudine asserts that the problem is not as great here because of the height. She insists that Rahambore is a healthier place than most, but she warns me about riding into the countryside. "Most unwise," she tells me.

May 25th

How bored I am with the society here. My only distraction is riding out on Byron II, smoking my *hookah* and taking Fudge for walks around the Fort. I have told them all that I lived at the Portuguese court in Brazil for two years and am therefore familiar with the tropics, but I fear they do not believe me. Why would the wife of a lowly officer have such a grand background? If they only knew.

I finally opened the letters I had received from my family. They had been put aside under a cushion until I could summon the strength to open them and receive the lectures and recriminations I knew they would contain. However, when I had unsealed them I lacked the courage to read them and put them in a trunk for later.

I am developing a love/hate relationship with India. Oh! The dirt and delight of this country, the colour and the squalor, the disease and the magnificence! Meryton scarcely seems to be in the same universe, and the stately halls of Pemberley do not compare with the marble and gold of the Maharaja's palace.

This evening while we were dining with the officers and their wives, the young officer who is Marshfield's envoy contrived to pass a note to me. It instructed me to ride out tomorrow with an escort to a certain place in the forest. I would then be taken to a secret pavilion. You can imagine, dear reader, the turbulence in my bosom when I read this note in the privacy of my room. During the meal I had contrived to direct glances at the panther god but he did not look in my direction. Indeed, he did not smile at all, merely listening with a serious expression to the senior officers sitting next to him.

His coat on this occasion was burgundy silk latticed with gold, and the buttons were small rubies. His turban was decorated with a ruby and diamond clasp. I could scarcely take my eyes from him and indeed, Mr M admonished me sharply at one point, "Your mouth is hanging open, my dear, most unseemly." He is intolerable.

May 27th

On the following morning I was waiting impatiently for my escort to arrive. Mr M had left for his soldierly duties and I wore my best riding habit and had doused myself liberally with jasmine perfume. We mounted up and set off for the forest. My heart was beating a drum-roll so loud that I was sure my escort could hear it, but his expression remained impassive as he signalled me to halt near an ancient tomb in a clearing in the forest. With a quick salute he rode away and I was left alone in some trepidation, listening to the murmuring vegetation and the loud cries of animals and birds.

Within minutes I heard a crashing sound, and to my amazement an elephant appeared, trampling through the undergrowth thus causing Byron II to shy away in fear. A splendidly decorated *howdah* was perched on the beast's back. I quickly tied Byron II to a tree and the *mahout* assisted me into the *howdah* and the waiting arms of the panther god.

"Madam," he exclaimed as we embraced. "I do not even know your name, but no minds!" His English was curious but enchanting.

"My name is Lydia, your Grace, your Highness," I burbled, unsure of the proper address. "Leeja," he replied. "You will be my English jewel."

We hugged as the elephant crashed its way to a nearby pavilion. With an imperious wave the *mahout* and his charge were dismissed. We were alone in the little open-air pavilion lying on a plinth covered with soft silk bedding. I held my breath and closed my eyes as my young god began to disrobe me.

A few hours later we were sitting side by side on the bier, naked except for the chamberlain's jewels that now decorated my body. Ropes of pearls and rubies lay on my bosom and a belt of emeralds and gold spanned my waist. Kymar Singh even removed his heavy silver wrist and ankle bangles and placed them on strategic parts of my person. The golden light sent shafts of mottled sunshine through the trees and into our pleasure palace. "Now we drink sherbert," the chamberlain announced, and a pitcher and drinking vessels were produced from a basket set nearby. "Then we make love again," he commanded. How can one describe the pleasure of love-making with a dark golden being, half-man, half-panther?

When our idyll was over, I was transported back to the clearing and I rode Byron II back to the fort in a daze. Nothing seemed real to me for some time, and Mr M remarked on my attitude, believing that I had a touch of the sun. The officers' wives again warned me of the dangers of riding alone in the forest but Mr M does not discourage me. Perhaps he continues to hope I will be eaten by a tiger. Adelaide took one look at me and said I looked "fair discombobulated."

I was still in a daze when, that evening, we attended a ball at the fort. Usually I love to dance, but the absence of Kymar Singh made the evening insupportable to me. The Indians consider dancing disgraceful for respectable women and only the *nautch* girls perform it. Later, Mr M edged away to gamble with the young officers. They play for very high stakes here, two guinea points at short whist and one hundred guineas on the rubber frequently. Mr M will be ruined, if indeed he is not so already. When I returned to our quarters Adelaide said that she and a native servant had killed three large scorpions after their evening meal.

CHAPTER
THIRTY-SEVEN

June 19th

An enchanted three weeks followed in which the panther-god and I contrived to meet every day in our usual place. I had allowed myself to be swept away on a tide of passion and romantic dreams, dear reader. My susceptibilities are well-known, but I defy any woman not to be overwhelmed by my golden man. The wives of the garrison are all a-twitter about him, gossiping ceaselessly and paying markedly more attention to their appearance.

It was not unknown for memsahibs to have discreet affairs with certain Indian gentlemen, and the menfolk were known to take Indian wives and even concubines. The famous Colonel Gardner, related to a titled family in England, has married a princess from the royal family in Delhi. Nevertheless, these events were not commonplace and I wondered anxiously whether anyone had connected my rides into the forest with Kymar Singh's absences from the fort. But whenever the green Eden of the forest closed around me and the little pavilion appeared in the distance, I forgot everything but the pleasures awaiting me. On this particular day I was given a surprise.

"We will go to the lake, Leeja," Kymar Singh told me. "It is beautiful there with water-lilies all around and a boat awaits us." The small tiger-headed vessel was poled by one of the chamberlain's servants and as we moved slowly through the water-lilies, we lolled on the cushions, abandoning ourselves to sensual delights. Kymar Singh pointed to a log on the lakeside which suddenly began to move. It was a crocodile, one of the many infesting the lake.

Later we returned to the pavilion where I was wound in a vivid pink and gold sari and a coil of large pearls and diamonds was wound around my neck. "You are made more beautiful," my lover told me in his strange, endearing English. As the days passed he showered me with gifts, Cashmere shawls, saris and jewellery, more precious gems than I had ever seen, but I could not keep them in the fort. They remained with the chamberlain until the time when I could collect them unobserved.

I had told Kymar Singh all about my trials with Mr M, and he had casually offered to have him killed! "Do not be afraid — it will be an accident only," he told me. I hastily explained that that would not do at all. I became quite agitated and he drew me close, kissing me passionately.

Another hour of bliss must have passed before I found myself riding back to the fort. I had been away three hours. Surely someone must have noticed? Instead, I found Adelaide waiting in detective mode.

260

"Have you noticed, madam, that Mr M's things are being moved?" I confessed that I had noticed little these past weeks. My mind had been on other things, cocooned in a love-in-the-mist haze.

"His things is all packed up but he isn't goin' anywhere," she remarked. "*No one* is goin' anywhere; we've just arrived. Why is he packing his things . . . and why did he do it himself? There are plenty of servants here."

"I cannot imagine," I told her. "Perhaps his debts are now so great that he is attempting to sneak away by moonlight, although I cannot think how he will accomplish it." We both paused to contemplate a vision of Mr M sneaking off through the wild countryside on a purloined camel at midnight. Perhaps he might even try to steal Byron II — perish the thought. I fingered my three rows of pearls nervously.

Adelaide vowed to watch the fellow closely, "as you are otherwise engaged, madam," she said, giving me a meaningful look.

It was true: Kymar Singh and I had discussed the future. He explained to me that our idyll could last only for a few weeks. Then he must return to the Maharaja in Jaipur and resume his duties. Because he knew my story, he would be the means to ensure my escape from my meaningless liaison. The jewels would ensure my welfare and he would provide an escort to Bombay.

I had grown to love many aspects of India, but I knew my future could not be in this land. The thought of leaving my panther-god was intolerable but inevitable. This might be all I could expect in this life

— snatched, brief encounters of delight. I wept a few tears and was enclosed once again in my god's embrace.

I rode back to the fort through the orange-red flame-trees contemplating how I would unshackle myself from Mr M. Little did I know that he would save me the trouble. My last sight of Kymar Singh was in public. He invited some of the garrison to a cheetah hunt, and to my surprise and embarrassment I was included. Ten people were assembled, some on elephants and some in carts. I could see that the wife of the garrison commander was offended by my presence, but I cared little. Kymar Singh's hunting leopard was in one of the carts with his handlers. When they removed the cap from his eyes and released his chain, the beast turned and placed his forepaws on the handler's shoulders.

I held my breath knowing that the animal could have torn out the man's throat, but he simply jumped down and sped off into the forest. Several antelope were brought down but I did not enjoy this sad spectacle. I sat in Kymar Singh's *howdah* forcing myself to avoid his gaze for the last time. The commander's wife made stilted conversation with him.

CHAPTER
THIRTY-EIGHT

June 21st

When we returned to the fort, the soldiers were assembled to bid farewell to the chamberlain. His gorgeously attired escort rode out of one of the seven great gates, with Kymar Singh at its head in a red satin coat blazing in the sunlight. I watched him leave with a horrid dead feeling in my heart.

It was only after the procession had departed that I became aware of some turbulence in the European ranks. A senior officer took me aside and asked me sternly where my husband was. I remembered then that Mr M had not been among the assembled officers. I protested that I had not seen him that day, having left early for the cheetah hunt. I explained that my husband (how I choked when I used those words) must have returned late last night and had decided not to disturb me.

"I assumed he had slept elsewhere," I told the officer and his aides. I could not understand the knowing looks they gave each other. Then I was told that Claudine, my erstwhile friend, was also missing. The expression on her husband's face was murderous and I was told that the two were presumed to have left together.

When I returned to our quarters and told Adelaide, she said it all made sense.

"They must have been planning to run off together. That was why he packed his things. He thought you would not notice, madam. He once told me you were so bemused you must be losing your wits!" I was surprised he had noticed anything. We met so rarely.

Who could have imagined that Claudine and Mr M would make an alliance? She, the wife of a senior officer, so respectable and upright. Mr M, of course, is not married and has no scruples whatsoever as I have reason to know. Later, I discovered that Claudine was wealthy in her own right. My false spouse would not have set his cap at her otherwise. We do not know how they managed to flee the fort by night. Help must have been given to them, guides bribed and animals used. Byron II was still safe but some of the military horses were missing. They were later found at a staging post. I do not know what retribution will follow from the Company — desertion and mutiny are punishable by death, no doubt, but Mr M, like the cat, has nine lives. I would not be in Claudine's shoes for anything.

I am regarded as an object of pity — and of suspicion — in the garrison. They "cast camel's glances" at me, as the local saying goes. Perhaps they think I aided and abetted the pair, but that is absurd. What would I have gained from such a startling action? Of course, in reality, I would have been only too pleased to help get rid of them. Mr M had not taken anything of value because there was nothing to take. I was wearing my pearls, and Byron II would have been a liability for them.

The Commander of the Fort was kindness itself. When I told him that I wished to leave as soon as possible, he arranged an escort, and Adelaide and I departed a few days later after perfunctory farewells. I heard mutterings that Mr M owed a great deal of money to various officers.

June 27th

We were escorted to Jaipur where we were offered accommodation in the palace, arranged by Kymar Singh. My trunk full of valuables was delivered to me, and plans were made for our journey to Bombay. I bade farewell to my lovely Byron II and told Adelaide to pack the *hookah*. We left for Alexandria where we spent a pleasant week or two admiring the classical ruins before embarking on a French vessel bound for Marseilles. Fudge accompanied us.

I thought it wise to leave India as soon as possible, but I had no wish to embark from Calcutta on one of the Company's ships, full of Company officials. When we arrived in Bombay I sent off a letter to Selena by a fast ship leaving that very day. Perhaps she will receive it before I arrive back in Europe.

August 10th

My Dearest Selena,

I have finally achieved my desire to escape from Mr
Macaulay and return to Europe! The strangest things can
happen here. I had become friendly with the wife of one of
the senior officers, Mrs Claudine Hetherington. She has
been in India for two years and she kindly gave me useful
information about life here and how it can best be lived. I
had not thought that she had any ulterior motive other than
friendship. How mistaken I was!

It appears that she cultivated me in order to get closer to
Mr Macaulay. They formed a secret alliance — improbable
as it may seem. They observed the utmost discretion; I am
sure that no one here, myself included, had the faintest
notion of what was going on.

Of course I was somewhat distracted myself, having
formed a close friendship with Another. I will tell you more
about this when we finally meet again. I hope it will not be
too many months hence, dear friend. Due to the generosity
of Another I have been well provided for and I can now
effect an escape from India. Mr Macaulay and his inamorata
have already disappeared under cover of night, to general
consternation.

The officers and officials of the Company were furious, as
you can imagine. In addition to his desertion Mr M had
many gambling debts. My position has been most
uncomfortable. I know that I was regarded as an object of
pity and of suspicion.

Fortunately, Adelaide and I were able to leave for the
journey to Bombay in haste, where we will embark on a

ship for Alexandria. As I write this we are enjoying a few weeks of rest here before embarking on a French ship for Marseille. In a few months we will be in La Belle France once again. I expect to remain in Paris for a while. I do not think that it would be politic to return to my parents, or to Pemberley at this time.

I have told everyone that my husband died of the cholera. I beg you, dear friend, to repeat this news to anyone you meet who is likely to have known me. I doubt that Mr Macaulay will bother me again.

Before leaving the fort I received your letter informing me of your good fortune, which delights my heart. How wonderful that we may all be settled at last! At least, in my case I will be settled financially if not in any other way. As you said, dear Selena, the ways of Providence are unaccountable. Once more I am your dear friend,

Lydia Bennet Wickham

Our brief sojourn in Alexandria included a meeting with the British Consul who informed me that the movement for the abolition of slavery was gaining ground in England. This appeared to be his only news other than details of cricket games.

I wondered what was happening to dear Lord Byron who is still in Italy, no doubt. I recalled that we had almost met during my stay there. As I was drowning at the time and he was swimming nearby, it might have happened, but it was not to be.

August 17th

When we boarded the ship I wore black and told the captain I was a widow, my husband having died of the cholera. He was all sympathy and concern, even offering me his cabin for the duration. It will avail him little. I could not look at another man, especially a European, after Kymar Singh.

By the time we arrived on board I had successfully negotiated the sale of the jewels given to me by Kymar Singh. If the merchants were surprised to find such valuables being sold by a female and a *ferenghi* (foreigner) to boot, they did not demur. I received very high prices and I was told that some of the jewels were so fine they must have come from royal collections. I smiled enigmatically and said nothing. At last, I am financially secure.

I whiled away some of my time on the ship day-dreaming about Paris and its pleasures — the clothes, the food. I dreamed of pink tulle and lavender-corded silk, of Roquefort cheese and coquilles Saint-Jacques, of the Place des Vosges and the plane trees in the parks, of smoked salmon with dill crepes followed by chocolate mousse, and champagne with every course. And not a curry in sight!

News has come from recent arrivals that waistlines are dropping and the Empire line may be quite "passé" by the time we arrive back on the Continent. Standing on deck in a stiff breeze, a sudden lust for Provencal calissons overwhelmed me. Those almond paste sweets were a passion of mine when I was in Paris. I say nothing of this to Adelaide who will think I am losing my wits if she is not so convinced already. She can pass the time making alterations to my wardrobe.

At this point my maid handed me the two letters that have remained unopened since I left the fort. I returned to my cabin and stiffened my backbone to read the missives from Lizzie and my mother.

My Dear Lydia (Lizzie writes)

You may be sure of the continuing warmth of my affection for you despite the shameful circumstances of your departure from Pemberley. These violent exits are becoming commonplace with you, are they not?

We heard that you are now in India with your husband. Naturally, we were all horrified to hear of the *Tanjore*'s shipwreck and greatly relieved to hear of your safe deliverance when it was announced in *The Times*. I hope, dear sister, that you have become reconciled to your husband and that you will deal tolerably well together. After all, Mama and Papa manage this. It is not given to everyone, sadly, to be as happy as Darcy and I — and also Jane and Mr Bingley. (Much gritting of teeth on my part when I read these lines.)

A husband who is a gambler is indeed a burden but let us hope that his employment with the East India Company will prevent him from any further excesses. (Hah!)

I trust that in due course you will be able to return to England. You will be welcome at Pemberley whenever you wish. Do not think harshly of my husband. He is concerned for your welfare and sends you his good wishes.

I am your own sister,
Elizabeth Darcy

What am I to make of this? I cannot imagine that Mr Darcy has changed his opinion of me — or of Mr Macaulay. How unhappy he will be if I return to Pemberley like a homing pigeon — and once more a widow! Surely there cannot be any more curates to dangle before me. I threw the letter down and turned to my mother's lavender-scented pages.

Dearest Lydia,

I am considerably vexed to learn that this letter will not reach you for many months. Why must you go so far away? I am sure that Mr Macaulay could have joined a regiment somewhere in Southern England where we might have had the pleasure of an occasional visit from you.

Is India insufferably dull? I hear the climate is insupportable and that few can bear it for more than two years if, indeed, they do not expire before. When I confide my fears to Mr Bennet he dismisses them with his usual flippancy. It is most vexatious. He declares that Mr Macaulay will probably meet with a fatality in the near future and you will be able to return home. I pray, dear Lydia, that you do not meet with any tropical misfortune.

Mary and Kitty are well but there are no beaux on the horizon for them. Mr Bennet makes no effort on their behalf. He will not consider a trip to Brighton.

My poor nerves are quite worn down and I am often prostrated with anxiety, especially when I think of you, dear child, in that dangerous land. I trust you are kept safe from leopards and tigers and other fearsome creatures?

Jane and Mr Bingley are well but, sadly, they have not been blessed with offspring. Is there any hope of issue from your union, my dear? If this should happen you must return immediately to England for the sake of your health and that of the child.

I have not visited Pemberley for some time. I confess I find Mr Darcy's gaze somewhat ferocious, but Mr Bennet and your uncle are frequent visitors and they are made very welcome. It is all somewhat strange and vexatious. I would greatly enjoy seeing my two little grandsons. However, there is also the chance of meeting that dreadful Lady Catherine de Burgh whom I would wish to avoid at all costs.

Write soon and tell me of your situation. Fondest love from

Your Mama

Dear Mama, she will never change. As for Kitty and Mary they will be fortunate if they secure a penniless clergyman apiece. I have other things to occupy my time on this voyage. I must prepare a report for Captain Marshfield although I have little to interest him, or His Majesty's Government. I shall certainly not be divulging details of my *affaire du coeur* with the panther-god.

August 21st

Last night when the passengers were at dinner I chatted to a French gentleman, Monsieur Audemars. When I spoke of my adventures in Brazil and India (carefully edited) he exclaimed that I should certainly write about them because they were so fascinating. He told me of a

French aristocratic female who has written a memoir of her frightful experiences during the Terror of the French Revolution and her various escapes from capture.

This led to a mention of my Gothic novel which remains close to my heart. It still lies in its locked box among my belongings. Fortunately, it was discovered in the trunk salvaged from the shipwreck. I told Monsieur Audemars that I had considered publishing the book privately. After all, I now have the means to do this. He was most encouraging, even offering to put me in touch with someone who would translate the book into French. This would be a coup indeed! He advised me to use a masculine pen name for the sake of propriety. I am a respectable widow, after all. Mr Macaulay's ridiculing of my novel still rankles.

When we arrive in France we will make our way to Paris. I have heard that the great violinist Niccolo Paganini is in the city. I have always wanted to hear him play. They say he is a great gambler and has sold his soul to the devil; a man after my own heart.